"We need to talk about that kiss."

"Which one?" Zoe asked cheekily.

"Be serious," Ryan admonished her. "You know what I'm talking about. The day we got a little carried away."

"You're going to sit there and *dissect* our kiss?" She didn't bother to keep the shock out of her voice. She remembered that kiss—no, make that series of kisses that ended with her almost melting into a puddle at his feet. "So you're never going to kiss me again?"

He nodded. "In that way."

"Which way?" she demanded. "The way a man kisses a woman when he feels something for her? The way you kissed me a couple of days ago and we both burst into flames?"

"Yes," he said, sounding as if trying to convince himself.

Dear Reader,

Spring cleaning wearing you out? Perk up with a heart-thumping romance from Silhouette Romance. This month, your favorite authors return to the line, and a new one makes her debut!

Take a much-deserved break with bestselling author Judy Christenberry's secret-baby story, *Daddy on the Doorstep* (#1654). Then plunge into Elizabeth August's latest, *The Rancher's Hand-Picked Bride* (#1656), about a celibate heroine forced to find her rugged neighbor a bride!

You won't want to miss the first in Raye Morgan's CATCHING THE CROWN miniseries about three royal siblings raised in America who must return to their kingdom and marry. In *Jack and the Princess* (#1655), Princess Karina falls for her bodyguard, but what will it take for this gruff commoner to win a place in the royal family? And in Diane Pershing's *The Wish* (#1657), the next SOULMATES installment, a pair of magic eyeglasses gives Gerri Conklin the chance to do over the most disastrous week of her life…and find the man of her dreams!

And be sure to keep your eye on these two Romance authors. Roxann Delaney delivers her third fabulous Silhouette Romance novel, *A Whole New Man* (#1658), about a live-for-the-moment hero transformed into a family man, but will it last? And Cheryl Kushner makes her debut with *He's Still the One* (#1659), a fresh, funny, heartwarming tale about a TV show host who returns to her hometown and the man she never stopped loving.

Happy reading!

Mary-Theresa Hussey

Mary-Theresa Hussey
Senior Editor

Please address questions and book requests to:
Silhouette Reader Service
U.S.: 3010 Walden Ave., P.O. Box 1325, Buffalo, NY 14269
Canadian: P.O. Box 609, Fort Erie, Ont. L2A 5X3

He's Still
the One

CHERYL
KUSHNER

SILHOUETTE *Romance*®

Published by Silhouette Books

America's Publisher of Contemporary Romance

To my mother, Shirley Kushner,
and my sisters, Terry, Maureen, Robin and Randi.

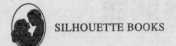 SILHOUETTE BOOKS

ISBN 0-373-19659-8

HE'S STILL THE ONE

Copyright © 2003 by Cheryl Kushner

This edition published by arrangement with Harlequin Books S.A.

® and TM are trademarks of Harlequin Books S.A., used under license.
Trademarks indicated with ® are registered in the United States Patent
and Trademark Office, the Canadian Trade Marks Office and in other
countries.

Visit Silhouette at www.eHarlequin.com

Printed in U.S.A.

CHERYL KUSHNER

trained as a journalist and is an award-winning writer and editor who has worked for several major newspapers in a variety of jobs—including news reporter, features writer and entertainment editor. She moved to New York in 1999, where she's the arts and entertainment editor for *Newsday*. The best part of her job, she says, is spending her nights at the theater on Broadway.

An avid romance and mystery reader, Cheryl has been writing fiction since 1993. She was first published in 1998. *He's Still the One* is her first book for Silhouette Romance.

Cheryl loves to hear from readers and can be e-mailed at CherRW@aol.com.

Dear Reader,

I'm a bookaholic, and there's nothing I enjoy better than spending time with a captivating romantic story.

I'm also a journalist, and back in the mid-1980s I was assigned a feature story about the growing popularity of romance novels. I bought dozens of books as part of my research and found myself totally fascinated. I read, read some more and was hooked.

A few years later, I started writing fiction, and it seemed natural that I turn to writing romance. Not only do I get to create spirited heroines and to-die-for heroes, but I also get to make up their quotes!

Zoe and Ryan, the heroine and hero of *He's Still the One,* have known each other since they were children. But even the best of friends can find themselves at odds, and sometimes friendships can be fractured so badly they seem impossible to repair. It's been ten years since Zoe and Ryan have spoken, and their first meeting doesn't bode well. It takes a wedding, and some unusual circumstances, for them to see they are truly meant for each other.

I'm proud to be a member of the Silhouette Romance family, and hope that you enjoy Zoe and Ryan's story. You can contact me at CherRW@aol.com.

Happy reading!

Cheryl Kushner

Chapter One

Zoe Russell had created hundreds, no thousands, of scenarios that had her face-to-face with Ryan O'Connor once again. None, however, had her wearing mud across her cheeks and heavy metal cuffs around her wrists.

She looked at her shackled hands, and tried not to wince at her twenty-five dollar manicure gone wrong. Zoe had no idea what Ryan was doing back in Riverbend, but it appeared for the moment he was all that stood between her and freedom. Showing any sign of weakness would be a mistake. He needed to remember Zoe Russell wasn't a woman to be pushed around or trifled with.

Zoe squared her shoulders, took a deep breath, and letting it out slowly, walked to the front of the cell keeping her gaze locked on his. "This has all been a terrible misunderstanding."

Ryan cocked a brow, rubbed his index finger along his chin. Yep, she could see that the all-too-sexy cleft was still there. Along with the little scar from a baseball thrown awry. He rocked back on his heels, smiled. "That's what all crooks say."

Oh, and that smile, bracketed by dimples that still sent shivers down her spine. The little stubble across his jaw didn't hurt, either. The man sizzled sex. Zoe steeled herself. *No weakness.* Especially not in front of the man she'd once considered her best friend— the man who'd broken her heart even if he hadn't realized it at the time. Hadn't she promised herself she wasn't ever, *ever* going to be taken in by his smile again?

She wouldn't think about what her hair must look like, or that a decent burial—not dry cleaning—likely would be the fate of her designer denim overalls. Forget about making a fashion statement. She was wet, tired, hungry and late for her dress fitting for her sister Kate's wedding.

And from the uncompromising coplike look on Ryan's face, she also was in big trouble. She still couldn't understand why she was the only person arrested at the senior citizen's rally. All she'd been doing was her job, interviewing the protesters, thinking she might have a good story for *Wake Up, America.*

"Shouldn't you be catching criminals in Philadelphia?" She winced at the petulance in her voice.

"I've discovered that the more interesting—" he paused and threw her a pointed look "—criminals visit Southern Ohio."

"I'm not a—"

"Save it for the judge. I've read the police report. Resisting arrest. Punching an officer…"

"He tripped and fell."

"Then you wrestled with him in the mud."

"He handcuffed me."

"Before the both of you landed flat on your faces in the fishpond. Rumor has it that's going to be the front-page color picture in tomorrow's *Riverbend Tribune*."

She took a deep breath to steady herself, trying not to imagine how much damage a photo like that could do to her TV career. And took another deep breath because seeing Ryan had shook her to the core. "As usual, you've got your facts wrong."

"So, enlighten me Ms. New York City TV star."

"I would rather eat snails."

"There's a new French restaurant in town." He paused. "Want me to check and see if they have take-out?"

Her stomach rolled. She couldn't stand the slimy things. And he knew it. "No," she said faintly. Then she steeled her voice. "But thank you."

"Guess it's pretty hard to look and sound haughty when you're dressed in mud." Ryan smothered a grin, but barely. Oh, if she only had these handcuffs off she'd wipe that silly, sexy grin right off his face!

Patience had never been her strong suit. She closed her eyes, mentally counted to ten. "If you're not going to help me, go away." And opened them when she heard his full-bodied laugh.

With a shrug, he started to do as she asked. Then

he paused, turned, and cocked a brow in her direction. "Nah." He shook his head and walked away.

"I know my rights," Zoe shouted after him. "I want my phone call. And my lawyer. I want to talk with the *person* who's in charge here!"

"That person—" Ryan turned to face her "—would be me."

She stared at him, trying hard not to let him know he'd caught her off guard. Again. But inside she was reeling. Ryan O'Connor was in charge of the Riverbend Police Department? The last she'd heard—not that she'd been paying attention to any gossip about Ryan—he'd received some commendation for heroism and was headed for the top-cop spot in Philadelphia.

So what was he doing back in Riverbend? It wasn't as though she cared...or did she?

She had to let him know she meant business. She held out her cuffed hands. "You have no grounds to arrest me. I didn't break any laws. I want these off, and I mean *now*."

"Actually, I do have grounds. You disturbed the peace. Something, I recall, you're very good at. The key's at the bottom of the pond," he said with an exaggerated patience that didn't fool her. She just knew he was enjoying her predicament. "My deputies are searching for it."

"And you're not guarding the master key?"

"They tell me it was lost the day the jail opened. That would be...let me think...some twenty-five years ago."

She tried to keep calm. "What about a locksmith?"

He shrugged. "Closed. It's Friday, after five o'clock. Riverbend isn't New York City. We don't do 24/7." With a smile that indicated he was anything but apologetic, he disappeared around the corner.

"Wait! Where do you think you're going?" She awkwardly raked the bars with her handcuffs. The resulting noise sent shivers through her teeth. "We're not finished here. You can't just walk away. Ryan! Get back here!"

She was sure she heard him chuckle. Otherwise, she got no response. Not that she expected one. Great. She was being held hostage in her hometown jail, and it appeared her jailer was none other than the last man on earth she'd ever ask for help.

It had been ten long years since she'd seen him. But she'd never been able to erase him from her thoughts. Now—suddenly, unexpectedly—he plops back into her already complicated life and for just a moment, a brief ridiculous moment, she felt tempted to ask him the one burning question left unanswered for the past decade.

She considered it a miracle he hadn't listened when she demanded that he get back here. Lord only knows what she would have said and how he would have responded.

Zoe gazed around the eight-by-twelve-foot cell. About as much room as her upper West Side studio apartment. And with about as much warmth. The single cot with its regulation flat pillow and scratchy gray blanket screamed uncomfortable. The tiny-screened window barely allowed in a stream of sunlight, let alone any fresh air.

"And let's not forget the fashionable iron bars on the windows and doors," Zoe muttered as she paced the cell once, then paced it again before flopping down on the cot.

She turned her face into the pillow and tried not to worry about how she felt as much a prisoner in her outrageously expensive apartment as she did here. She wasn't going to think about New York now. Or her job as on-air columnist at *Wake Up, America* that she loved, but which was slowly beginning to eat away at her heart and soul. Not that she'd ever admit that to any of her colleagues or friends. She found it hard enough to admit to herself.

They all thought she had the perfect life. They celebrated her most recent success last month with a party at the hottest club in the city when she was promoted from mere entertainment reporter to the coveted weekly morning spot on *Wake Up, America*. People she hadn't heard from in years had called or e-mailed when they'd read about that party in the "Sunday Styles" section of the *New York Times*. She'd been thrilled when her mother had sent her the front page *Riverbend Tribune* article on her promotion, with the less-than-original headline Local Girl Makes Good.

She had achieved the goal she'd set when she'd graduated from college six years ago. She worked and lived in Manhattan. She had plenty of twenty-something friends and acquaintances. And because of her work she was considered a celebrity of sorts.

But she couldn't put out of her mind how New York City's tabloids had referred to her last week when the network announced she would be hosting a two-hour nighttime entertainment special in addition to her appearances on *Wake Up*: Ms. Perky Goes Prime Time. The phrase still distressed her. Whoever called her perky hadn't been paying close attention to her recent *Wake Up* segments.

She wasn't just promoting glitz, glamour and celebrity faces. She sought out serious stories, about real people and how they were dealing with their complicated lives. She knew more than she wanted to about complicated lives. Like her own.

Zoe sat up and took a deep breath. If only her colleagues on *Wake Up, America* could see her now. They'd never recognize the woman they'd only seen as perfectly polished, not when she remained handcuffed, wet and wearing mud from head to toe, behind bars in a tiny jail cell in the one place she'd sworn she'd never return to. If she discovered another woman in a similar situation, Zoe was certain she'd find a way to turn that woman's tragedy into a two-minute TV triumph for *Wake Up*.

She looked down at her mud-caked hundred-dollar tennis shoes in dismay. Whatever had possessed her to buy them? They were expensive, trendy and downright uncomfortable. They were perfect for New York, but so out of place here in Riverbend. Was she out of place in Riverbend, as well?

Zoe shook her head to clear it of troubling thoughts. Oh, what she'd give for a cup of latte and one of Andre's full-body massages. She needed her wits about her to convince that certain someone with the sexy cleft in his chin and perfectly dimpled smile that she was the victim of an unexplained case of amnesia.

She could pretend she'd never taken part in the senior citizen rally, tussled with the police, ended up in the fishpond, been arrested or found herself the subject of Ryan O'Connor's penetrating blue-eyed stare that probed too deep and saw too much. While she'd happily parade all her triumphs in front of him, she'd prefer to keep her missteps to herself.

She buried her face in her hands. This visit home for her sister's wedding, Zoe knew instinctively, was going to be the longest two weeks of her twenty-eight-year-old life.

A smart man would have dived into the fishpond and searched for the key himself. Or cajoled the locksmith to make another. And paid her bail himself. Then Ryan could have opened the cell and hustled pretty Zoe Russell out the front door of the Riverbend City Jail and out of his life.

Ryan O'Connor was smart. He was clever. And very, very shrewd. All these traits had saved his butt more than a few times during his years first as a homicide, then vice detective in Philadelphia. So the fact Zoe was still behind bars told him maybe he wasn't as smart, as clever or as shrewd as he thought.

Physically, she was all he remembered: tall, slender, with green eyes that sparkled like the emeralds she now wore on her fingers and her ears. Oh, and that unforgettable curly red hair. At one time he'd considered her his best friend—and the bane of his adolescent existence. But he had no idea *who* she was now.

She used to disdain showy jewelry, had been afraid to get her ears pierced and had worn only a simple pearl ring belonging to her grandmother. This woman was much too polished, much too savvy and much too sophisticated for his taste. That's the way she appeared on morning TV. Not that he'd ever admit to sitting down and watching her, of course.

If he'd met Zoe for the first time today, he'd have been polite, but never taken the time to get to know her past that first hello.

He could tell himself she was the last person he expected to see back in Riverbend. But that would be a lie. He knew she'd be coming to town for Kate's wedding. He just hadn't figured on seeing her this soon. Her unexpected appearance in his jail had left him unprepared. Little Zoe Russell—no, make that grown-up Zoe Russell—couldn't keep out of trouble. It was one of her most endearing and most exasperating traits.

You can't just walk away.

Except he had. The words were still a punch to his gut. He'd heard them from her before. And still he had walked from his friendship with Zoe, his life in Riverbend and, inevitably, from his youthful marriage to Kate, which had been a mistake on both their parts. Six months ago he'd walked away again, his decision, although not his choice, from almost a decade of fighting Philadelphia's crime and watching it fight back until he was losing more than winning. More than anything, Ryan hated to lose.

He dropped into the oversize oak chair, planted his feet on top of the scarred desk and, through the open door of his office, surveyed the calm scene before him. The phones were mercifully quiet. His dispatcher sat at her station reading the latest issue of a celebrity magazine. The community affairs liaison was reuniting the Johnson boy with his runaway puppy.

"Ah, suburbia," he muttered. "A far cry from the mean city streets. I will be happy here." *I will be happy here.*

He leaned back in his seat and closed his eyes. And prayed his mind wouldn't replay that deadly night in Philadelphia. A drug sting gone wrong. He'd taken a bullet to the side, and through the haze of pain he'd seen his longtime partner, Sean, go down with one to the back.

Everything that had mattered to him had changed that night. He hadn't been as strong, as heroic, as he'd needed to be. Even though everyone told him he'd been all those things. The professionals also told him the nightmares would go away. As usual, they were wrong.

"Uh, chief?"

He slowly opened his eyes. Jake, his childhood friend, his number one deputy and the man who bravely had wrestled Zoe Russell into an arrest, stood before him, wet and muddy but with key in hand. Ryan rubbed the tired from his eyes. "Care to explain how a peaceful protest about the new senior's park ended in complete chaos?"

Jake poured his lanky body into the chair across from Ryan's desk. And grimaced as he dripped mud and water all over the floor. "Zoe started interviewing people. Once they realized who she was, they pushed and shoved to get her attention. I was trying to get to her and we slipped and ended up in the pond."

"Were the handcuffs really necessary?"

"Jeez, Ryan, she punched me. I did it as much to protect me as her. I had no choice but to arrest her." Jake wiped the key clean before placing it on Ryan's desk. "I haven't forgotten what it's like to be on the other end of Zoe Russell's hard right."

"You were eight and she was six," Ryan reminded him dryly. "And you'd just stuck a tadpole down her bathing suit. In that very same pond, too."

"Yeah, well, the tadpole was your idea." Jake's scowl turned into a wide grin. "Should I let her out? Or maybe throw away the key for a few more hours?"

"Let me handle her." Ryan tossed the key into the air and caught it. "Everything under control at the park?"

"The protest fell apart peacefully once we had Zoe in custody." Jake chuckled. "You should have seen Flora Tyler. Demanded that Zoe pose for a picture with the senior citizen group. Bet it will make the front page of the *Tribune*."

Ryan laughed. "That's what happens when a celebrity comes to town. Have you called Kate about bailing her sister out?"

Jake nodded. "Gave me an earful. Mumbled something about how she hadn't talked to Zoe yet, and asked if she could beg a second favor."

"She expects me to post Zoe's bail," Ryan guessed

and wasn't surprised to hear Jake still chuckling as he walked out of the office, closing the door behind him. Ryan fingered the key he'd pocketed. Too bad the key wasn't a coin, and he could toss it into the air, leaving it up to fate to determine whether he would—or should—grant Kate's second favor.

Because he knew exactly what Kate wanted him to do. She'd been dropping not-so-subtle hints since she'd set her wedding date last month. Make peace with Zoe. At least for the next two weeks until the wedding was over and Zoe headed back to New York. There was nothing in the Ryan O'Connor rule book that said he had to go back and rehash the last ten years. That was history. And since the incident in Philadelphia, Ryan had become very good at ignoring the past.

As Ryan grabbed his checkbook and headed for the court offices next door, he didn't want to consider whether or not he was strong enough to turn a blind eye to the woman Zoe Russell had become.

Zoe's limited stock of patience had run out.

She didn't appreciate being ignored. She didn't appreciate being locked in this tiny jail cell—still handcuffed—for more than an hour. It felt like days.

She shook her hands to clear them of the numbness, then winced as the cuffs jangled heavily against her wrists. Not her jewelry of choice. Somehow, some way, she'd see that Ryan paid for not having a master key to these cuffs. She'd like to think that if their roles had been reversed, she'd graciously have called the locksmith, even if his workday was officially over.

Zoe tried to curl up on the cot. The lumpy cot. With a pillow missing its crucial foam or feathers. She hoped Kate got here soon to bail her out. She couldn't take much more of Riverbend's unique blend of hospitality.

She closed her eyes, then immediately opened them when the image of Ryan's face appeared. Those perfect features. Chiseled chin. Deep-set blue eyes. Thick blond hair that seemed kissed by the sun. It had been ten years since she'd last seen him in the flesh. Photographs and family home videos didn't count.

He looked better than she remembered, sexier than she'd imagined possible. She tried to picture him at sixty-five, potbellied, gray-haired—no, make that *bald*—limping down Main Street chasing after a criminal, banned from driving a car because his vision was so bad.

She smiled at the image she had created of a not-so-perfect Ryan O'Connor. Too bad men like Ryan usually aged like fine champagne, not cheap wine. She stood and paced the tiny cell. Why was it taking him so long to find that key? And who did Ryan think he was dealing with, anyway, claiming Riverbend was not a 24/7 town? She knew full well that locksmiths everywhere *lived* for being called after hours so they could charge outrageous overtime fees.

"He owes me a phone call," Zoe muttered. "I should call the locksmith, just to prove him wrong. Ryan! I want my phone call!"

When Ryan didn't materialize, Zoe shouted out his name again. She heard footsteps and braced herself. But it wasn't Ryan. It was Jake.

"Uh, Zoe," Jake said with a wariness Zoe could understand. After all, they had tangled in the fishpond and ended up wet, dirty and slightly shaken by the encounter. And she'd punched him, a fact she deeply regretted. "Uh, Ryan hasn't let you out yet?" He glanced right, then left, everywhere except at her. Finally their gazes met.

Zoe motioned him closer until they stood face-to-face. "You don't want to be the one who tells me he's found the key but hasn't unlocked the cuffs."

"Can I…I mean…is there something else I do can for you?"

"You can accept my apology for hitting you. And I want my phone call."

"Apology accepted." Jake warily handed her his cell phone through the bars, then reddened in embarrassment when she waved her still-cuffed wrists in front of his face.

"I can hardly punch out numbers while my hands are otherwise occupied, Jake. Maybe," she said gently, "you could help Ryan find the key."

Jake slowly backed away. "I'll get Ryan."

"You do that," Zoe said, trying to keep her voice bright.

She watched Jake disappear around the corner. He was tall, like Ryan. Had an athlete's body, like Ryan's. Handsome features, including deep-set blue eyes, also like Ryan's. But when she stood face-to-face with Jake, she felt nothing, there was no sizzle between them. Unlike the sizzle that had unexpectedly snapped, crackled and popped when she and Ryan had stood on opposite sides of the jail cell door.

What she feared most was caring for Ryan again, maybe even falling head over heels for him again, because in the end, he'd pick up and leave.

As she impatiently waited for the man to appear, Zoe pondered why the Ryan she'd met today had sizzled and every man she'd dated during the past year in New York had fizzled. She'd chosen them, she admitted wryly, because they hadn't sizzled, hadn't captured a portion of her heart and soul. And when they left, as a'l the men in her life inevitably did, she'd been left whole and emotionally untouched. And alone. Very, very alone.

But that was preferable, she told herself, than to be left alone *and* heartbroken. The way she'd felt when her father left, when Kate left, when Ryan left. Okay, so the all-too-sexy Ryan O'Connor could still made her sizzle. Nothing wrong with that, as long as she didn't act on it.

Zoe lay back on the cot, letting her eyes drift shut again. This time the image was of the night of her high school graduation. Her parents were seated as bookends to the two empty chairs in the otherwise packed Riverbend High School auditorium. She'd never forget that June night when her world had turned upside down. Her parents had announced they were separating. And Kate and Ryan had eloped. She'd been eighteen, hurt, crushed, devastated and determined never to forgive any of them, especially Ryan.

She was twenty-eight now. Long ago she'd made peace with Kate, and accepted but still couldn't claim to understand the reasons for her parents' divorce. But she hadn't let herself answer *why* she still felt the sting of Ryan's betrayal.

Maybe, she admitted to herself, it was because she didn't want to accept that their friendship, which had meant the world to her, hadn't been important enough to him.

The sound of approaching footsteps—very different male footsteps from Jake's—helped clear her mind. She waited until she heard the cell door open before she raised her head to look at him. Keep it light and breezy, she reminded herself. If he sizzled, she would definitely ignore it.

"So nice of you to visit," she said brightly as he stepped inside the jail cell. "I'll ring for the coffee or tea while you tell me what you've been up to the past ten years."

"Ms. Zoe Russell, always ready with a joke."

She sat up, held out her cuffed hands. "I don't consider this situation funny at all."

Ryan joined her on the cot. If it surprised Zoe that she let him, she could tell by the expression on his face she'd surprised Ryan even more. "Don't you think it's time you let me loose?"

"Jake found the key." Ryan fumbled with it before unlocking the cuffs. He cleared his throat. "I see you every morning on TV."

"Oh?" Zoe stood, stretched her aching arms over her head. Out of the corner of her eye she watched as Ryan tidied up the cell, folded the blanket, punched up the pillow. "You watch *Wake Up, America?*"

"Not exactly. The only way I could get our community liaison here at seven in the morning was to install a TV so she could watch her favorite show. Even without the TV, though, it'd be hard to miss you.''

Her voice chilled. ''I don't know what you mean.''

''Magazine ads. TV spots during prime time. I'm not criticizing. Just observing how you got what you wished for. Fame. Fortune.'' He cupped her shoulder and turned her to face him. ''A chance to ham it up in front of millions of people.''

''Is that what you think of me? That all I care about is being a celebrity? I'm a serious journalist. I worked hard to get that spot on *Wake Up, America.*'' She paused, raising herself to her full height of five feet seven inches, but she still fell short of Ryan by almost half a foot and had to tilt her head back to meet him eye-to-eye.

She stared up at him, fascinated by the specks of gold in his blue eyes, the way his dimples deepened when he smiled. For one inexplicable moment she was torn between wiping that smile off his face and kissing him senseless. Then, thankfully, Ryan cleared his throat and broke the moment.

''You're standing on my foot.''

Zoe glanced down to see her left mud-splattered sneaker on top of his right shiny black boot. She stepped back, horrified to discover large chunks of dirt on his toe.

Ryan took his handkerchief out of his back pocket and Zoe immediately reached for it. After a slight tug-of-war she sighed and let it go. Ryan brushed the dirt off her cheeks and from the tip of her nose. That brief touch made her insides quiver and the goose bumps run up and down her arms. His smile made her weak in the knees. Looking into those blue eyes made her want to kiss him. Which would be wrong. Which would be totally inappropriate. Which would be a giant mistake.

Which was why she had to get away from Ryan before she did something they'd regret. But it was getting harder and harder to ignore the way Ryan O'Connor made her feel.

"I think I've got the worst of it," he finally said. "Your bail's been paid. You're free to go."

Zoe stepped out of the cell and into freedom. She walked down the hallway to the reception area, aware that Ryan followed in her wake. Aware that he stood a few discreet steps behind her as she signed for her personal belongings. As she swung her tote back onto her shoulder, she tossed a nod in Ryan's direction. "Is there something else?"

"I'll walk you home," Ryan said.

"That's not necessary."

"Consider it part of my job." He swung an arm lightly around her shoulder. Couldn't he feel the sizzle between them? "I want to make sure you don't take any more detours."

They silently walked the three blocks to Kate's house. She sneaked a glance at Ryan and wondered what life would have been like for Ryan, Kate and her if…if they'd never *left* Riverbend.

And found him staring at her, intently.

"Am I interrupting something?" a female voice called from the other side of the screen door.

"No!" Zoe and Ryan, their gazes locked, spoke in unison.

"I think I am." Kate Russell opened the screen door and ushered Zoe inside. "But I'm happy to see my maid of honor and best man are speaking once again."

Chapter Two

"Ryan O'Connor is your best man?" Zoe dropped onto the queen-size bed in Kate's guestroom, adjusted the pillows behind her back and propped herself up against the wrought-iron headboard. "First you conveniently forget to tell me he's back in town. Next you drop the best man bombshell. What other important news are you keeping from me?"

"Why would you think I'm keeping stuff from you?" Kate set two glasses of iced tea on the nightstand before wrapping a blanket around her shoulders and curling up next to Zoe.

"Because you know I hate surprises." Zoe vigorously toweled her hair. Twenty minutes in a hot shower had done wonders to restore her body but not her mood. Only Ryan O'Connor disappearing into oblivion would do that. "You should have called the minute he crossed into the city limits."

"You wouldn't have listened to me," Kate returned sweetly. "Your exact words were, 'Don't anyone, anywhere, at any time, mention that man's name to me ever again.'"

"That's hardly the point." Zoe scowled again at Kate's snicker. "And I can't believe I'd say something like that. I was eighteen. Nobody in their right mind pays attention to what eighteen-year-olds say."

"Ryan did." Kate said quietly. "So did I."

Zoe fumbled for a response. When she looked at Kate she felt she was looking into her own soul, although the sisters were as different as night and day.

Zoe had always despaired that with her red hair and fair skin she burned rather than tanned, while Kate, with their paternal grandmother's exotic dark looks, seemed to keep a deep honey color even in winter. While Zoe was tall, slender and could eat without gaining an ounce, Kate was shorter by several inches with an hourglass figure and had to watch every calorie. Growing up, Zoe had been impulsive, Kate cautious.

As adults, Zoe had become the more conservative, while Kate seemed to be throwing all caution to the wind. Which might explain, Zoe considered as she gazed around the room that had once been hers, why Kate was marrying a man she barely knew.

She walked over to the single window, now framed by sheer white cotton panels. Zoe vividly remembered the day she'd climbed out the window into the tree and somehow lost her balance. A gangly twelve-year-old Ryan, who'd just moved in next door, had carried her inside to treat her scraped hands and knees. She'd been eight, and had developed a full-blown case of puppy love, which had turned into hero worship when they were teens. She'd lost count of the number of times she'd climbed down that tree and joined Kate and Ryan on their adventures.

She and Ryan had climbed the tree together the night of her sweet-sixteen birthday party and he'd kissed her. Zoe hadn't thought so at the time, but she'd come to realize he hadn't meant it as a romantic kiss, but one of friendship and affection. But for a starry-eyed Zoe, the kiss had been a turning point. Her feelings about Ryan began deepening into something more than a childish puppy love.

Zoe wouldn't dwell on the past. Couldn't. Because then she'd have to answer questions she'd prefer to ignore. Questions that had bounced around in her thoughts from the moment she'd seen Ryan O'Connor on the other side of that jail cell door.

Zoe tossed the towel at her sister. She saw the worried look in Kate's eyes and chose to ignore it. "All I'm saying is that it would have been nice if someone, like you, had kept me in the loop about Ryan."

"Nice?" Kate chided.

"Prudent," Zoe conceded. "It was a shock to see him again."

"So prudent you would have found some silly excuse not to be my maid of honor? Stop blaming Ryan for something that was both our faults. We never meant to hurt you."

Zoe winced at the truth in Kate's words. She'd never told anyone she'd had a king-size crush on Ryan. That she'd dreamed one day he'd see her as more than a pint-size pal. That, at the time, she hadn't seen Kate and Ryan's teenage elopement for what it was, as a form of rebellion. And that after Kate and Ryan divorced, Zoe and Ryan had never been able to regain anything resembling their once-close friendship.

But Zoe was just as certain if she'd known Ryan was back in town, she'd have come home for the wedding. Ten years ago, the night of her high school graduation, she'd heaped the blame for all her pain on Ryan's wide shoulders. He'd let her. He'd never offered an excuse, or tried to shift the blame.

Zoe settled at the foot of the bed and reached for one of the glasses of iced tea. She sipped and sighed. Lots of sugar. Just the way Mom made it. "How long did you say he's been back?"

"A few months."

"As police chief? Philadelphia get tired of him and take away his key to the city?"

"You'll have to ask Ryan for the details because he's told me next to nothing. But I gather it was the other way around. Maybe you should take the time to get to know the man he's become." She looked at Zoe slyly. "He's not seeing anyone."

"Not interested," she said quickly. "What makes you think I would be? What is it about brides-to-be? Is it your mission in life to fix up every single female you know? Am I so lacking in male companionship that you're offering me your *ex-husband?* And that's supposed to cheer me up?"

"I want you to be as happy as I am."

"Having Ryan be your best man isn't a step in the

right direction," Zoe said dryly. "You've only known Alec Carmichael a few weeks. Three dates and you're engaged."

"A few months," Kate corrected. "Time is irrelevant when you're in love. Alec is perfect for me. Ryan's perfect for you."

"I'd rather not have this discussion. Ever."

"It's time we did." Kate tossed her a look that brooked no argument. "Ryan and I were never meant for each other. And who's been complaining she's always a bridesmaid and never a bride?"

"What I meant was…" Zoe scowled. "It's not nice of you to bring that up."

Kate laughed. "I'm your older sister. Nice has nothing to do with it. I just want what's best for you."

"Then stay out of my love life."

"Just pretend you met him today for the first time."

Zoe rolled her eyes. "I was dressed in mud. He was dressed in perfectly pressed tan chinos and a T-shirt that hugged his muscles. Yes, I noticed how good he looks. He called me a crook and I insulted him right back." *And I wanted him to kiss me.* Zoe's breath caught in her throat. Her eyes widened and her mouth dropped open. There was that traitorous thought again.

Kate briskly clapped her hands. "Besides, Ryan meets the Zoe Russell list of dating qualifications. He's single. He's breathing. He's straight. He's here."

"That's low, Kate, even for you." Zoe shuddered, determined not to try and follow what passed for

Kate's logic. Let Ryan O'Connor back into her perfectly ordered life? No way. Never. She wasn't that desperate, wasn't ever going to be that desperate, for a relationship.

She held up her glass. "No, iced tea the way Mom makes it is perfect for me, but I know the sugar she dumps into it is bad for me." Her voice caught in her throat. It was important Kate understood her feelings and didn't do something Zoe would live to regret. "I'm not one of those women who need a man to make her complete. I'm happy with my friends and my family."

"Ryan's always going to be a part of our family. Even though we've been divorced longer than we were married. You were good friends once. You can be friends again." Kate reached for Zoe's hand and gently squeezed. "At least talk to him. Clear the air between you."

When hell freezes over. "Soon as I see him."

"Promise. It's important to me."

Zoe sighed. The always tenacious Kate wasn't going to let go. "Okay. One little talk. Just for you."

Kate wrapped her in hug. "You won't regret it."

I already do. Zoe knew she owed it to Kate to be the best maid of honor she could be. She'd be careful so that she wouldn't run into Ryan. If she did, she would be—she wracked her brain for a word—pleasant, she'd be pleasant.

"And then," Zoe said brightly, "I won't have to see him for the next two weeks, until I'm forced to stand across the aisle from him on your wedding day."

Meanwhile, she wouldn't think about what it might be like to kiss Ryan, be the recipient of his sexy smiles or caress his dimples. But she was intrigued about the haunted look on his face when she demanded to know why he'd left Philadelphia. She'd get to the bottom of that soon enough.

"There is one more thing you should know..." Kate's voice trailed off.

From the ominous tone in her sister's voice, Zoe wasn't sure she was ready for the one more thing. "And that is...?"

The sound of male voices downstairs had Kate running to the top of the staircase. Zoe followed, curious.

"Anyone home up there?" called a deep voice Zoe knew she hadn't heard before.

"Alec?" Kate frantically brushed her hands through her hair, checked her appearance in the hall mirror. "Zoe's finally arrived. And there's a problem with the caterer."

Zoe sighed, returned to the bedroom and closed the door. She just bet the *one more thing* Kate had failed to tell her had to do with Ryan. She slipped out of her terry-cloth robe and into a pair of well-worn jeans and a *Wake Up, America* T-shirt. Her eyes caught the mud-caked tennis shoes she'd tossed on top of the clothes hamper. She gingerly picked them up by their shoestrings and dropped them into the waste can by the bureau. No time like the present to get rid of unnecessary luxuries.

And no time like the present to meet her future brother-in-law. A quick glance into the hallway mirror told her she was as presentable as she could possibly be, under the circumstances. Maybe her cheeks were a bit too flushed, her eyes a bit too bright, but she'd spent twenty minutes in a hot shower.

She jogged down the stairs into the living room to find her sister wrapped in the arms of a dark-haired man a few inches taller than Kate. The look on Kate's heart-shaped face was one of a woman deeply in love and secure in the knowledge that her feelings were returned.

Kate quickly made the introductions before spiriting away Alec so they could discuss wedding plans. Zoe walked into the kitchen. She wasn't surprised to see Ryan seated comfortably at the kitchen table with an open pizza box in front of him.

"Why are you here?" Zoe asked crossly before she had a chance to check her emotions. "I think we've spent enough time together for one day."

"Best man stuff." He cocked a brow, surveyed her up and down several times before turning on that devastating smile. "You clean up well."

"How *nice* of you to notice."

"Almost didn't recognize you without the mud." He glanced down at her hands. "Or without the cuffs."

"I save the more sophisticated look for prison." She sighed, took a step back. Ryan stood and took one step forward. He was much too close. She thought about her promise to Kate. Make peace? Not tonight. "Go home, Ryan. I'm too tired to play clever repartee with you."

Zoe yanked open the refrigerator door with more force than necessary. She pulled out two beers. It appeared Ryan wasn't going home. She tossed one bottle in his direction. "No reason to let pizza with the works go to waste."

He caught the bottle before it made contact with his head and gently set it on the table. He eased himself back into one of the high-back oak chairs. "Your aim hasn't matured along with the rest of you."

Zoe wanted to snarl at him. She really did. It wasn't good manners that kept her from doing so. It was that marching band with its percussion section at full volume that had just begun rumbling through her head.

She closed her eyes and rubbed her temples trying to ease the pain. *Just pretend you met him today for the first time.* Right. If life were simpler, and Zoe years younger, she'd happily take Kate's advice. Ryan had grown from a gangly cute teenager into a devastatingly handsome man. She knew Kate would ignore her plea that she wasn't interested in Ryan, and would still find a way for them to spend a lot of quality time together during the next two weeks. She wondered if she'd survive the experience.

Zoe ordered herself to keep the conversation light but on point. She needed all her wits about her. "Kate thinks we should talk. Clear the air. Put the past behind us." *Date.* No, dating Ryan O'Connor was not a viable option. Not now. Not ever.

Then he smiled. And Zoe's heart beat a tattoo. She thought back to earlier in the day, and the effect he'd had on her senses. From the moment they'd met, she'd been on the defensive. It was past time to turn the tables and put Ryan O'Connor in his place. "Let's play Truth or Dare."

"Truth or Dare. And I'll live to regret it." Ryan's smile didn't reach his eyes. "I admit I've followed your career because I take pleasure in your success. You tell me why you've treated me like a pariah the past ten years."

She sputtered as she fought to swallow a gulp of beer.

"I *know* why." The patience in his voice didn't fool her. He was angry and trying hard to keep his emotions under control. "I'm not an idiot. I just need you to tell me why. Actually, *you* need for you to tell me why."

Zoe swallowed the gulp, but it was a few more seconds before she finally found her voice. "I'm not going to let you reduce the last ten years of my life into some sixty-second commercial for..."

"You wouldn't have offered up Truth or Dare if you didn't have something important to say to me."

She hated it when he was right. When they were teenagers, playing Truth or Dare was the way they dealt with sensitive issues they'd rather not—but knew they had to—talk about. She didn't want him to be right. She didn't want him to be a handsome, sexy and available man.

Zoe wanted him to be going bald, with bad skin and a paunchy stomach. With a nagging wife and several snot-nosed brats who drove him crazy. She wanted him to be a thousand miles away and not upsetting her already much too complicated life. But he was here. And she had no choice but to deal with him.

He looked so comfortable sitting at her family's

dinner table as though he'd always had a place. He'd always belonged there, and when he'd gone, he'd left a hole no antiseptic could heal, no Band-Aid could begin to cover. She resented him for making her feel anything, even anger and most especially desire, for him. But she didn't know what to say to him.

"You've always underestimated me. You've never taken me seriously. You've never really known me. How would you like it if I ripped into your life?"

Ryan's expression hardened. He stood, leaned over the table so they were face-to-face, mere inches apart. "There's nothing to *rip into*."

She kept her gaze locked to his. "I don't agree. Let's start with why you're sitting in the police chief's chair in Riverbend when all you ever wanted to do was chase crooks in the big bad city."

"That's none of your business." His voice was devoid of emotion.

"You left." She challenged him to deny her words as she abruptly changed the subject and answered his Truth question. "We were friends, Ryan. Friends don't desert one another."

"I graduated from college," he said patiently. "I moved to Philadelphia to take a new job."

"You weren't there on the most important night of my life."

"Guilty as charged. We missed your high school graduation. But Kate and I had other things on our minds."

"You eloped! Why?"

"I'll tell you if you answer why our marriage sent

you into such an emotional tailspin that you neatly and deliberately cut me out of your life.''

"I can't answer that question.''

"Can't,'' he said quietly, "or won't. It was never about me marrying Kate. Or our moving to Philly. It's always been about your father.''

Zoe's heart pounded in her chest. She felt each painful breath as she slowly exhaled, then inhaled then exhaled again. She'd thought the day couldn't get any worse. She was wrong. "Leave my father out of this. You don't know anything.''

"Your parents separated. I know it was a painful time for you, but they did what they thought best. Kate was hurting, too. And I was reeling after my parents were killed in that stupid car accident,'' Ryan said softly. Now she heard the pain in his voice, and tried to harden her heart against it.

"Kate got me through the grief,'' he said. "We were young, impulsive and thought with our hormones.''

All Zoe remembered was that night she'd thought she'd lost three people who'd meant the world to her. And now, here Ryan stood, ten years later, trying to push back into her life and opening wounds she'd only been able to messily bandage.

He slid the plate across the table. Their hands touched. Zoe felt the sizzle and tried to pull away. Ryan kept her hand in place with his for a moment more. "Kate and I were smart enough to recognize almost immediately that we were totally wrong for each other. We married on impulse. I'll always love her but I'm not in love with her. Your parents divorced because they realized something was missing in their marriage. You were hurting. I let you blame me then. But I won't let you continue to blame me now.''

Her parents had divorced. Zoe hadn't wanted to listen to their explanations of why. All she knew was that her comfortable family life had been destroyed. With her father moving to California, and Kate and Ryan married and living in Philadelphia, Zoe had been left alone that summer to deal with her emotionally wrought mother and her own feelings of abandonment.

It had taken many months before Zoe had been able to have a cool but cordial relationship with her father. She was afraid to trust her feelings, afraid of being hurt again. She might have aged ten years, but she didn't feel any differently today than she had back then. And Ryan O'Connor was a life-size reminder of all she had lost.

''Well, so much for clearing the air between us.'' With all the energy she could muster, Zoe brushed past Ryan and calmly walked out of the kitchen, through the living room where Kate and Alec were now cuddled on the couch and out the front door.

She paused at the end of the walkway and turned around. Ryan stood silhouetted in the doorway. Zoe started walking, not expecting, but hoping he'd call out, or come after her and finally admit, after all these years, that he'd been wrong. With a heavy heart, Zoe trudged down the street. The wind had picked up and Zoe was certain she heard it whisper, ''little coward,'' as it swept past her.

When she came to the street corner she stopped, gazed around and realized she had nowhere to go except home. Not New York, but the cozy bungalow on the aptly named Division Street, filled with memories she'd prefer not to deal with.

Ryan rested his forehead against the closed door. "You sure bungled that one."

Ten years ago, Ryan had given up the right to call Zoe a friend. When he'd acted rashly following his parents' deaths, and his elopement with Kate certainly was rash, he hadn't been thinking of anyone but himself. Of anything but his anger, his hurt, his pain. Zoe's feelings never entered into any equation.

And he'd regret that the rest of his life.

But no matter how all grown-up Zoe was, there was no way he was getting involved with her. She was practically his little sister! No matter how strong the temptation, she was, he decided firmly, off-limits.

There had been several women in his life. He was, after all, a normal healthy man with a normal, healthy sex drive. But he hadn't allowed himself to get close to any one woman emotionally for any length of time. He wasn't proud his emotional barriers flashed a red alert whenever a relationship looked like it might get too serious.

The excuse was always the same. He was a vice cop. His life was dangerous. He couldn't ask anyone he cared for to share the uncertainties. Except he wasn't a vice cop any longer. His life wasn't filled with danger or uncertainties.

Still, he wasn't ready to dive into any depth of

emotional waters. He wasn't afraid, just wary of not being able to live up to someone else's expectations. It was hard enough, he thought with a frown, to live up to his own.

He turned to find Kate standing in the archway, worry written all over her face.

"Your talk with Zoe cut short?"

"How could you forget to tell Zoe I'm the best man."

"Oops." She shrugged slightly. "It's not that big a deal."

"It's a big deal to Zoe. You deliberately didn't tell her."

Kate winced. "I had hoped to ease into it. That was before you locked her in jail."

Ryan wisely decided to ignore that last comment. "Were you going to pull her aside moments before the wedding ceremony began and say, 'See that guy in the black tux? He's our best man and you're walking down the aisle with him. You recognize him? That's Ryan O'Connor. Your ex-best friend.'"

"Yes."

"Not funny, Kate."

"I wasn't trying to be funny. I'm still waiting for you to promise you'll get along with Zoe over the next two weeks."

When he didn't respond she poked him in the chest. *"Promise."*

He nodded curtly. "I'll do my part. You might want to remind her it takes two to end a war."

"Zoe understands," Kate said with exaggerated patience. "You just don't know her the way I do. She feels things differently than you or I do."

"I'm not even going to begin to try and make sense out of that statement." He glanced at his watch. "I need to check in at the station. And, Kate, remember that Zoe and I are like oil and water. We no longer mix. And I have no intention of getting involved with her. So don't play matchmaker. It will just blow up in all our faces."

Ryan heard the click of the door close behind him, and a few murmured words between Kate and Alec before the porch light flicked on ostensibly for Zoe's return. He reached into his pocket for his cell phone, punched the three-digit code that immediately connected him with the police station. Once the night dispatcher assured him all was quiet, he hurried down the walkway, turned right and stood on the sidewalk in front of the house next door. The house that had once been his home. And would be again.

He stared intently at the For Sale sign, remembering how he'd seen it shortly after he'd returned to Riverbend six months ago. Winding his way through the backyard, Ryan found the garden of roses his mother had so lovingly tended. He was foolishly pleased to see them still in bloom.

A rustling sound in the bushes behind him put Ryan on alert and he quickly raced to the front yard. And was surprised to see Zoe standing on the sidewalk. Her face, lit by the light of the moon, looked troubled.

Ryan settled on the top step that led to the front porch. And remembered his promise to Kate. "Join me," he invited, and when she did, he didn't fail to notice she kept as much distance between them as she could.

"I really don't want to talk to you."

He heard the firmness in her voice. "Fine. We'll just sit here quietly."

"I always wanted to live in your house."

Ryan was smart enough not to ask why. He remembered all the shouting coming from the house next door, the slamming doors, her mother crying. "I'm just remembering the first time we met." He chuckled. "Even back then you left a strong impression."

He'd plopped down onto the window seat and was gazing into the yard next door where a pixielike redhaired girl, partially hidden by a gnarled oak tree, watched him from her bedroom window, a curious look on her face.

"I was just happy, thinking I now had someone new to play with," she said dryly. "And was crushed you were a boy."

She'd climbed onto one of the thick tree limbs and when their gazes connected, they played a silent game of stare down until she unexpectedly laughed, then disappeared from view.

"I panicked when I realized you'd fallen out of the tree."

"My pride was bruised and battered," she said.

"And you never shed a tear."

"I was afraid to cry," she told him. "If my parents had heard us, they'd know I'd climbed into the tree. I was certain the next time I saw that tree it would be as firewood."

Then she laughed. "But the next morning you made a real impression when you lost control of Webster, and he crash-landed into my wading pool."

"It was always a toss-up as to who owned who," Ryan said, remembering the day his golden retriever puppy had plopped into the swimming pool. Eight-year-old Zoe, buried beneath twenty-plus pounds of dog, had cried, not because she was hurt, but because she was worried that Webster had been injured.

His expression darkened as he recalled another day, the one when he'd buried his parents in the cemetery around the corner and then came to defiantly hammer a For Sale sign, much like the one in the yard now, into the ground. Webster's loud bark had accompanied each pound, until Zoe had come to the rescue of both man and dog, ordering him into the shower and taking Webster for a much needed walk.

From the doorway, he'd watched the two of them flash down the street, wishing he could always be with them, with her, with anyone, anywhere but in this house, alone.

A long silence stretched between them, until Zoe stood abruptly. "I'm sorry Truth or Dare got a bit out of hand."

"Yeah." He scrubbed his hands down his face. "It's been a big-drama day for the both of us."

Ryan watched as Zoe jogged across the yard and into the house. He slowly walked to the edge of the yard, stopping at the For Sale sign.

And for a moment, a brief moment, he wished he could turn back time.

Chapter Three

Ryan ran hard, the soles of his shoes slapping the pavement in tune with the irregular beat of his heart. Fast. He was running much too fast. His target managed to keep about one hundred yards ahead, just out of reach, then suddenly turned the corner. Ryan moderated his pace and by the time he reached the alley, he was breathing hard but steady. He drew his gun. There was no escape at the other end of the alley. He stepped forward, pivoted and aimed—into a suffocating deep-red mist. He coughed. Couldn't breathe.

Something wet seeped through his canvas shoes, and he looked down to find himself standing in a puddle of blood. He couldn't see his target. He couldn't see Sean. But he saw a faint image of Zoe, heard her call his name, and watched as she helplessly reached out to him, her hands drenched in blood. What was she doing here? Her image dissolved into the mist. He heard a voice mock him. *You're too late. Too late.*

A loud *pop!* jolted Ryan out of his chair. He'd closed his eyes for a moment and had been treated to a full-blown nightmare. He sprinted across his office to the lobby area of the police station he saw both his dispatcher and Jake standing in the entranceway shaking their heads.

Ryan went into his big-city detective mode. "What happened?" he demanded. "Anybody hurt? Why are you two standing there? Get outside and see what's going on."

Jake turned away from the door. "I know what's going on. Henry Larkin's car backfired again. Been ticketing him for more than a month now, telling him to get that muffler fixed."

Ryan sucked in a deep breath, held it briefly before slowly exhaling. "Tell him the next time I hear or see his car I expect it to have a new muffler that sounds like a purring kitten, not like a round of fire from a sawed-off shotgun."

He went back to his office and watched through the window as the eighty-year-old Henry Larkin waved in his direction and slowly drove around the square, his car halting, then backfiring every few hundred feet, a cloud of exhaust following its path.

He dropped into his chair, exhausted, which explained why he'd merely closed his eyes and drifted off. Sleep had been elusive last night. He'd risen with the sun. Taken a jog. Back at the apartment he'd stirred up the dust on the furniture. Still feeling restless, he'd showered, then driven around town aimlessly until he found himself at the police station. He'd decided to catch up on paperwork that was so boring, he'd fallen asleep in his chair.

He closed his eyes and called forth the memories of the first part of the dream. Minutes before sunrise he'd sat parked in front of the Russell house, waiting. Through the front window Zoe had seen him. She'd thrown open the front door, raced down the walkway and into his arms. They'd kissed. A kiss so light, so gentle, that it had him silently begging for more.

And so he'd kissed her again, holding her tightly against him, feeling the sizzle and the heat between them, their hearts beating as one. He'd felt alive for the first time in months. Then he'd woken up, feeling frustrated, irritated and impatient.

He told himself, no he *ordered* himself, not to think of Zoe as anything other than a little sister. This dream didn't bode well for the immediate future. Not when his gut and groin tightened by just dreaming about her. He was not going to give in to temptation. It wouldn't be right. It wouldn't be fair.

He sighed, scrubbed his hands down his face. He should go home, try and get some rest. He knew Zoe hadn't tossed and turned all night. He'd bet a week's pay she'd slept soundly, like a rock, just like when they were children. Back then, nothing, short of the ringing alarm clock pressed to her ear, could wake her. He expected the same was true now.

And if she'd dreamed of him at all, he thought grimly, she probably had him handcuffed and locked in jail. Which was probably where he belonged, considering the racy thoughts he'd been having about her.

He dug into the bottom drawer of his desk and found the photo frame he'd stashed there the first day on the job. He set the picture of him and Sean, taken the day they'd become partners three years ago, on his desk. Two men, so different physically that they'd been tagged Night, for Sean's black Irish good looks, and Day, for Ryan's all-American boy blondness.

"I should have been there for you, buddy," Ryan murmured.

For a moment he considered what the police shrink had told him. Let the stress out of his life. Right. He didn't know what he would do with himself if he couldn't be a cop, even a temporary one in Riverbend. He needed to keep working so he could keep feeling, and if he was feeling, he told himself, maybe he could convince himself he was living, as well.

He pushed away from his desk and walked over to the window, surprised to see Zoe sitting on the stone edge of the fishpond where she'd made her big splash back into his life.

She wore faded denim overalls and a bright orange T-shirt that clashed with her red hair. On her it looked stylish, not garish. She appeared young, innocent and not the big-city sophisticate he knew she'd become, the woman he found himself watching each morning on TV, dispensing gossip and advice.

There was a subtle sensuality to her. He felt that familiar tightening, one that reminded him it had been a while since he'd been with a woman.

If sex was the answer, Ryan could have solved his problems months ago, as there were any number of women in Riverbend who would have slipped between the sheets with him for a night of mindless and, on his part, emotionless passion.

Ryan watched Zoe drag her hand through the water and smile. He found himself smiling, too, albeit sadly, wishing her smile was for him. But knowing it would be better for both of them that it wasn't.

Zoe brushed her hand across the water, and watched her reflection ripple as several large goldfish came up near the surface. One of them had pouty lips like Jeremy. Ugh. Pouty lips and a superior attitude made for a dreadful boyfriend. She was glad he was out of her life. She wasn't anxious to meet and date any more men like Jeremy.

She yanked her hand from the water, sending the fish scattering to the bottom of the pond. Her thoughts came back to Ryan. She smiled. Sexy lips, she decided, not at all pouty. But he definitely possessed a superior attitude. Her gaze shifted to the police station across the street and she swore she could feel Ryan staring at her. Except no one stood outside and it was impossible to tell if someone was looking through the slats of the window blinds.

Then, as though she conjured him with her thoughts, Ryan appeared in the doorway. A black T-shirt announcing he was one of Philly's Finest was tucked into black jeans that rode low on his hips. Definitely sexy.

Ryan O'Connor spelled danger with a capital *D*. She'd known it the moment she'd stood on the wrong side of the jail cell, facing him, that same sexy smile planted on his face. Those sexy dimples, that sexy cleft. The tousled blond hair that was a shade too long. *The you're-a-goner-if-you-stare-into-them-too-deeply blue eyes.*

Normally a sound sleeper, last night Zoe had tossed and turned in bed. Playing Truth or Dare had only widened the all-too-huge rift between them, Zoe thought as she warily watched him purposefully cross the street, a determined look on his face. A rift Zoe knew was one of her own making. She could attempt to deal with Ryan on her own terms for the next two weeks, or she could work on repairing their friendship.

They'd been best friends growing up, and Ryan had been her first love, even if he hadn't realized it. He'd treated her like a cherished younger sister, even when she discovered innovative ways to irritate him. She was, she thought with a hint of a smile, still finding ways to vex him, and as a grown woman found the present experience a heady one.

She was still attracted to him, and powerless at the moment to know how to end that attraction. Still, she ordered her heart to slow down, her palms to stop tingling and her feet to move her in the opposite direction before she made a complete fool of herself. The man obviously wasn't interested in her that way. Her heart and palms responded. Unfortunately, her feet did not.

He sat next to her, shoulder-to-shoulder. "So, soldier, how go the wedding wars?"

He could always make her laugh. "I needed a break. I've spent the past hour at the dressmaker being pushed, prodded and pinned until I was ready to scream.'' Still, she had to admit, even though the fitting seemed like a game of live-action paper dolls, the pale peach off-the-shoulder gown fit like a dream, surprisingly didn't clash with her red hair and brought out the emerald green of her eyes.

"So now it's on to the next battle?" Ryan's yawn muffled the question.

Zoe eyed him closely. "You look as though you didn't sleep a wink last night."

He brushed aside her concern with a wave of his hand. "I'm fine. How's Kate holding up?"

"Today she isn't happy with any of the catering selections she made yesterday," Zoe said dryly. "I imagine she and Alec are still deep in conversation about the merits of various canapés, pâté and finger sandwiches."

"Lesser decisions have been known to make or break a marriage," Ryan said gravely, although his smile tempered his words. "And how's your mother holding up?"

"She wisely stayed out of the conversational fray and volunteered to shop for party favors for the bride's lunch I just learned I'm hosting next weekend at the Café on the River." She sighed. "It's usually at this point that I realize how much effort it takes to be a bridesmaid."

"Maid of honor," he pointed out.

She shrugged. "Same difference. Not that I wish Kate and Alec would elope. Oops," she added hastily, seeing from the dark expression on Ryan's face that he also remembered the last time Kate had eloped. With him.

"Maybe you should get married and turn the tables on Kate."

Her smile wavered a bit. "Not ready to take that step. I'm following the New York single woman's dating mantra. Keep it simple. Keep it casual." *Don't lose your heart. Or let it be bruised.*

And that caution had her quickly saying goodbye and hurrying across the town square to The Party Shoppe, aware of Ryan's footsteps behind her. His pace quickened. So did hers. She stopped abruptly and he caught up to her, blocking her path.

"Why are you following me?" She tried to muscle past him, but he stood immobile, his arms crossed in front of him.

"Just making sure you get across the street safely. Wouldn't want to pull you out of the pond for the second time in two days." He smiled that devilish, sexy smile, the one that teased, that flirted, that knew exactly what it was doing to her heart rate, the smile she longed to wipe off his handsome face.

"Which is what?" Zoe asked sweetly. "Making a nuisance of yourself?"

He nodded solemnly. "Especially if it means ensuring your safety and well-being until after the wedding."

She rolled her eyes. "I don't need a bodyguard or protector. I haven't been away from Riverbend so long I can't remember the route from the party favor shop to the florist."

He opened the door and waved her inside. "Kate said…"

Zoe groaned as he brushed past her and meandered

through the store, hoping her mother was still there. "I can just imagine what she said." That Zoe should put the past behind her and get to know the man Ryan was today.

But would it hurt to take Kate's advice, take the time to know the man he'd become? Was she brave enough to take a chance?

She wished she could find a way to stop Kate's meddlesome matchmaking without hurting her sister's feelings or taking Ryan into her confidence. What would Ryan say if she told him Kate wanted to play matchmaker? He'd probably arrest them both. "I can't believe you'd pay attention to her ravings."

Ryan cocked a brow. "Your sister is one of the most sensible women I know. Besides, I promised."

"Promised what?" Zoe asked cautiously.

"For the next two weeks I'd do my best to get along with you, no matter how vexing you turned out to be. And that—" he held up his hand when Zoe started to reply "—if she was as smart as she pretended to be, she'd stop any matchmaking plans between us before someone got hurt."

It was one thing, Zoe thought, for her to be upset at Kate's matchmaking ploy, but yet another to hear Ryan say directly he wasn't interested in her in that way.

Zoe would have loved to argue the point further. But it was smarter, and safer, to nod in agreement, hoping Ryan would tire of whatever game he was playing and leave her alone. With just a few words he'd managed to knock the wind out of her sails. And maybe, just maybe, she'd spend the next two weeks putting all of her limited seduction talents to work and just prove Ryan O'Connor wrong.

When she realized her mother had come and gone she strode purposefully out of the store. Ryan followed but remained silent. He stuck to her like glue through all her remaining errands and up to her front door. He opened it, gently pushed her inside and handed her the packages. "I'll be in touch."

"That's not necessary." She eyed him warily.

"Just keeping my promise," he said softly through the screen door.

She watched as he strolled down the walk, whistling as though he hadn't a care in the world. Zoe, however, stood there motionless long after Ryan disappeared around the corner.

"Maybe *you* can talk some sense into our mother."

Zoe leaned against the doorjamb and watched in awe at the scene being acted out before her. Kate, wearing flannel pajamas, their mother, dressed in a silk pantsuit and pearls, were playing tug-of-war over an old apron. Not just any old apron, but one Zoe recognized as having been in the Russell family for years and declared, in a now-faded embroidered message, that the wearer was Not the Cook.

"I thought this kitchen was a mother-free zone," Zoe whispered in Kate's ear, distracting her sister just enough so that her mother, Penelope, with a quick tug wrenched the apron from Kate.

"I've been taking lessons," Penelope said archly. She smiled triumphantly as she tied the apron around her still-slim waist. She twirled once, then a second time, before returning to the stove. She picked up a spatula and turned over something Zoe thought vaguely resembled a pancake.

Penelope, Zoe thought fondly, was a terrific mother, but a lousy cook. She couldn't remember the last time her mother had successfully operated a major—or for that matter a minor—kitchen appliance. Once her daughters had been tall enough to see the top of the stove, they'd taken on the cooking, baking and cleaning chores. No more burned breakfasts, lunches or dinners. No more scalded coffee. She barely brewed drinkable iced tea, then doused it with sugar. It appeared as though this morning wasn't going to be any different.

Kate sank into a chair. "It's barely seven and this is the second batch of pancakes you've botched."

Penelope held out a sample to Zoe. It was flat—as a pancake to be sure—but burned to a crisp and looked as hard and as unappealing as a dirty rock.

Zoe shuddered. "Too early, Mom, for anything but coffee." She kissed her mother on the cheek, then grabbed a mug from the counter and started to reach for the pot.

Penelope beat her to it. "Let me do that for you, dear. I brewed it just the way you like it."

Zoe smiled faintly, and as soon as Penelope's back was turned, she poured half the contents into the sink. She took her cup over to the table, and slid into the chair next to her sister. The coffee would be either too strong or too weak. Either way, she'd attempt to drink it because Penelope had brewed it. Zoe sighed, propped her elbows on the table, rested her chin on her hands and watched her mother at the stove.

"Isn't this nice? It's been such a long time since we Russell women shared breakfast." Penelope plopped a plate on the table filled with flat hard rocks and something that resembled burned paper but smelled like burned bacon. She sat, and pushed the platter in Kate's direction. Kate gingerly pushed it toward Zoe, who picked up a slice of burned bacon and stared at it in fascination a moment or two before dropping it onto her plate.

"I don't eat big breakfasts anymore." Zoe slid the bacon into her napkin and her plate onto her lap, then leaned over the table and waved her hands in front of her mother's face. "Earth to Penelope Russell. Why did you drive fifty miles to make us breakfast?"

"I couldn't sleep," Penelope said. "So I decided to come over here and cook. Kate may own this house now, but I still think of this as my kitchen."

Kate nodded sagely. "That explains it."

"Explains what?" Zoe asked. She slowly sipped the coffee. A little on the strong side, but drinkable. She added some milk.

"Talk some sense into her," Kate groused.

"I'd be happy to. If I knew what you were yapping about." Zoe thought a moment. "This isn't about cooking lessons."

"More coffee?" When Zoe and Kate both shook their heads, Penelope poured a cup for herself then added enough cream and sugar to keep Zoe—as well as the entire population of Riverbend—wide-awake for days.

Zoe shot Kate a fierce look. "Have you two been talking about Ryan and me behind my back?"

"Not every conversation we have in this house concerns you or Ryan," Kate admonished her. She turned a worried look in Penelope's direction. "Maybe it's mother-of-the-bride jitters."

Penelope brightened. "Do you think so?"

"You never get jitters." Zoe got up from the table, stuffed the bacon-filled napkin into the garbage can and put her plate and coffee cup into the sink. On her way back to the table she stopped at her mother's chair, wrapped her arms Penelope's shoulders and kissed the top of her mother's head. "You're the calmest person I know." She watched her mother gulp down the cup of oversugared coffee, and then pour herself another full cup. "Except now. I thought you stopped drinking coffee."

"I've allowed some vices back into my life. I'm still young enough to enjoy them." Penelope patted her gray curls. "How would I look as a blonde?"

No way was Zoe going to answer that time bomb of a question. "You're drinking coffee again. Taking cooking lessons. Wearing pearls in the morning. What aren't you and Kate telling me?"

Penelope straightened her shoulders. "I've decided to start dating again."

"Dating? Mother, you're..." Zoe frantically searched her mind for how old her mother was. "You're almost sixty."

"I'm fifty-seven," Penelope replied, "and my friends say I don't look a day over fifty. I still have my figure and my faculties. Why shouldn't I enjoy what little time I have left? You two girls have careers. What do I have? Wednesday night bingo.'' She shuddered daintily. ''I hate bingo. Bingo's for people who have given up on life.''

''You told me you love your new condo in Cincinnati,'' Zoe felt obligated to point out. ''That you'd made new friends.''

''He's an old friend.'' Penelope smiled wistfully. ''Someone I never expected to see again.''

''That's all she'll tell me. And just who is this old friend?'' Kate asked. ''What do you know about him?''

''Everything *I* need to know. When the time is right, I'll tell you girls what *you* need to know.'' Penelope looked affronted. ''Did I ask Kate twenty questions when she announced she was marrying Alec? Ryan's known him longer than you have. And am I the last person in Ohio to learn you're keeping your maiden name?''

Kate sputtered a reply.

''I don't want to hear about how young women today can support themselves,'' Penelope continued, clearly on a roll. ''And have I ever asked you, Zoe, about all the men you must meet in New York City and why not one of them is a potential son-in-law? No, I have not.''

This time it was Zoe who was speechless.

''I blame you, Zoe,'' Kate said, ''for that series you did last month on *Wake Up, America*, the one about older singles joining the dating game. That's all mother and her friends at the condo have been talking about.''

"I loved that series." Penelope patted Zoe on the hand. "Gave us *seniors*—" she glared at Kate "—something to think about besides knitting booties for grandchildren we'll never have!"

"I vote yes on Mom dating," Zoe said, taking her mother's side mostly to irritate Kate. Penelope smiled her approval. Kate rolled her eyes. And then, as if on cue, the three of them laughed. "Go discuss wedding plans." Zoe began to clear the table and with a wave of her hand ushered the two of them out of the kitchen. "I'll finish in here."

She needed a few minutes alone to digest her mother's news. Zoe smiled to herself as she filled the sink and squirted dish detergent into the warm water. She could just imagine her mother's old friend. Silver-haired. Tall and lanky. Probably wore plaid trousers and a Polo shirt to bingo games where he convinced Penelope to play the five-dollar cards.

In all the years since her parents' divorce, Zoe couldn't remember Penelope mentioning being interested, or wanting to date, another man. She'd never offered a harsh word against Lawrence Russell after the divorce.

"We married too young, then grew apart," her mother had replied when Zoe had asked for a reason a few months after the divorce became final. Then Penelope had smiled wistfully, much in the same way she had today, and changed the topic of conversation. Zoe wondered even now if her mother had ever stopped loving Lawrence Russell.

During one of Zoe's early visits to her father at his new home in California, she'd persisted on knowing the reasons for the breakup. Her father, who had refused to get into any details about the marriage's failure, had agreed with Penelope's assessment. And never, in the years since the divorce, did he offer an unkind word about her.

Still, Zoe felt her mother had been wronged. And that Zoe and Kate had suffered for it. The divorce had made Zoe wary of men and their promises.

Her father wasn't expected in Riverbend until the day of the rehearsal dinner. And, as far as Zoe knew, her parents hadn't seen each other since the divorce. She only hoped that seeing Lawrence Russell at the wedding didn't upset Penelope. She supposed it was a healthy sign that her mother was interested in a man who showed some interest in her. Even if she wasn't ready to confide the details to her daughters.

Zoe had looked forward to spending these two weeks with her mother and sister. Her days in New York were anything but relaxing. Work, errands, more work. She had too little time lately for friends, dating, to see a movie or a Broadway show.

Too little time to enjoy life, the little voice in the back of her mind nagged, not for the first time. But for the first time the voice sounded just like Ryan's.

She'd been back in Riverbend a few days and he had invaded the sanctity of her childhood home, her thoughts about her work and her personal life, and now even the little voice she'd been able to count on to get her through life's daily ups and downs.

But what would have happened, Zoe wondered, if instead of getting up from the table in anger she'd yanked him to her and kissed him senseless? She was spending way too much time thinking about kissing Ryan. But at least she'd have thrown him off balance, which was the way she felt now.

Sleep hadn't come easy last night, nor had it been restful. Oh, why had she let her temper—and her emotions—get the better of her? Why had she stormed out of the house after a few of those truths had proved too painful to deal with?

She wasn't ready to deal with the reasons she was still angry with Ryan. Except they'd been friends. Best friends. And he'd broken that sacred trust between them.

She carefully washed, then rinsed the china cups and plates before setting them on the drain board to dry. How easy it seemed for Kate to fall in love with a man she'd known less than a few months. And how easy it seemed for her mother to announce her intention to start dating.

Zoe found that it was *not* easy to listen to her biological clock tick away while she tried to manage her brilliant career, deal with her nonexistent social life and not worry about what Ryan O'Connor thought of her. She'd deal with him during the time they were forced together as maid of honor and best man. And she'd flirt with him, too, if just to show him she could break through his wall of self-control.

Peals of laughter flowed from the living room. She heard *that* male voice, deep, rumbling and all-too-familiar. Ryan again. He kept turning up where and when she least expected him.

"Forget how to use a dishwasher?" He had come up behind her. He ran his fingers playfully through the soapy water, conjuring up all sorts of images Zoe knew she was better off *not* thinking about.

She scooped up a handful of soapsuds, knowing what she was about to do was fraught with the kind of danger she used to indulge herself in with Ryan when they were younger.

He had her loosely pinned to the sink, but she managed to turn and paint his face and the front of his T-shirt with suds. His look of surprise was worth the knowledge that he'd likely repay her in kind.

He wiped the suds from his shirt. "What was that for?"

"Just indulging myself." She laughed, and gathered up another handful of suds.

This time, Ryan was ready for her. He grabbed her wrist and slowly drew her to him.

"What are *you* doing?"

"Just indulging myself," he said so softly that Zoe wasn't sure she heard him correctly.

He surprised her with a kiss—of soapsuds. With his fingers he gently spread the soapsuds across her lips and chin. She shoved at his chest. Ryan let her go, his gaze troubled, as though he'd never seen her before.

Then he bolted—that was the only way she could describe an action so out of character for Ryan—out the back door.

Gotcha, she thought. Zoe pulled the stopper from the sink and watched the soapy water wash down the drain. And smiled.

Chapter Four

Zoe sat cross-legged at the coffee table in Kate's living room, keeping one eye locked on the TV screen as she furiously scribbled on the paper in front of her. The video of the rough cut of her first entertainment special had arrived via overnight delivery shortly before noon, and for the past hour she'd been watching it carefully, adding her suggested changes to the ones she'd received earlier in a phone call from her producer.

But she was finding it hard to concentrate.

She couldn't decide which was more distracting—Ryan's presence or his absence. She'd expected to see him Sunday for brunch at Kate's, after her sister made a big deal about inviting him. He'd accepted but was conspicuously missing. Later that afternoon, Ryan didn't show up for his weekly hoops match at the high school with Alec, who'd just shrugged off any questions about his wayward friend.

Not that she'd been seeking him out, but when she'd casually dropped by the police station yesterday afternoon, Jake would only say Ryan had taken a few personal days off. He'd be back, Jake had told her flatly, when he came back.

It had been on the tip of her tongue to ask where she could find him. *It's none of your business,* the little voice inside her head had scolded. Blissfully, the voice no longer sounded like Ryan's. It was just that Zoe had certain questions, certain expectations, not to mention certain thoughts that she knew she was smarter not to think about.

Like the kiss of soapsuds. What *was* she willing to risk to discover what he was up to?

Not her heart, that's for sure. He'd made it perfectly clear how he felt. Or had he?

On one hand, he told her he had no intention of getting involved with her when he'd outright dismissed Kate's matchmaking plans. Then he admitted he was proud of her and her accomplishments on *Wake Up, America.*

Here it was, Tuesday, and he'd kept his distance. Which probably wasn't a bad idea, since almost every conversation she had with Ryan turned into a sparring match. Why? And why did it mean so much to know the answers?

Stop thinking about him! the little voice now chided. *In less than two weeks, you'll be back in Manhattan, and you'll forget all about Ryan O'Connor!* Unfortunately, Zoe wasn't certain the little voice was right.

Zoe forced herself to think about her special and

forget about Ryan. Her program, she noted with some dismay, was scheduled to air between nine and eleven o'clock, the Friday night before Kate's wedding, eleven days from today.

She wasn't crazy about the time slot she'd been assigned, but hopefully with good promotion on *Wake Up, America*, including an interview with her via satellite from the network's affiliate in Cincinnati, and—she crossed her fingers—some good reviews from the TV critics, people would watch. And like what they saw.

She'd heard the network bigwigs would be watching closely. Which meant, she thought dryly, as she pressed the fast-forward button on the remote, her career was riding on the success or failure of the program.

She skipped ahead to a three-minute scene that was scheduled to close the first half hour of the program. The TV screen filled with the face of an up-and-coming young British actress, known by the singular name of Mia. During their long afternoon together, Zoe had learned more about Mia than she knew about herself.

Zoe had called in several favors in order to get Mia to agree to the interview. And the first tidbit she'd filed away was that the word *discretion* did not seem to be listed in the actress's personal dictionary.

Mia was a celebrity flavor of the moment, and there was good word-of-mouth on the actress's new movie—a romantic comedy about a twenty-something twenty-first-century Londoner who's magically transported to the nineteenth century and falls in love with a duke.

Zoe had tried—unsuccessfully as the tape painfully revealed—to keep the interview lively and on point. Her questions about changing male-female relationships through history were met by Mia's incoherent answers.

She watched Mia ramble on and on about falling in and out of love with unattainable men, including her most recent lover whom she never named but that every viewer would recognize as a powerful British political figure. No amount of editing, Zoe decided as she sipped from her glass of iced tea, would save the interview.

And no amount of mending, she thought sadly, could easily patch up her relationship with Ryan.

Zoe wasn't ready to admit to her mother or to Kate how much she missed Ryan's friendship. She couldn't stop thinking about him, or the romantic feelings she still had for him. Feelings that were growing, feelings that were making it difficult for her to look at Ryan and know he was determined not to feel anything for her, other than friendship. If even that.

It would be far easier to forget him if she felt nothing *for* him. That thin line people talked about that existed between love and hate took a great deal of emotion to maintain. Emotion Zoe needed to channel into building her career.

Unfortunately, she couldn't ignore him, not when members of her own family kept tossing him in her direction. Not when her obligation as maid of honor included dealing with Ryan in his role as Kate and Alec's best man.

If only…Ryan hadn't returned to Riverbend.

If only…he wasn't the best man at Kate's wedding.

If only…she wasn't feeling troubled over the fact that everyone she knew either was married, engaged to be married or at least dating someone that they might marry.

But there was no one special, no one special man, in her life. Despite what she'd told Kate, she was lonely, and she deeply longed for a special relationship.

If only…

She hit the pause button on the remote, freezing Mia's ramblings in midsentence. She shook her head, attempting to clear it of any thoughts about Ryan. And then she heard a slight buzzing noise.

She rose and followed the sound, wincing at it grew louder the closer she got to the kitchen. By the time Zoe stood in front of the screen door at the back porch, the sound had grown from merely annoying buzzing to teeth-chilling sawing.

She peered through the screen. Some man next door was chopping down her oak tree! The tree she'd found solace in as a child. The tree where Ryan first kissed her.

Dozens of branches had fallen, littering the lawn between the two houses. The tree killer's face was hidden by the branches he hadn't yet cut, and wouldn't—if Zoe had anything to say about it.

It took a moment for her to recognize the man as Ryan. He was memorable, especially stripped to the waist, wearing nothing but a pair of faded, paint-splattered jeans, ripped at both knees.

The blood rushed through her body. Then she felt foolishly faint. She grabbed the door handle to keep from sliding into a puddle of mush.

Superb was the only word she could think of to describe that body. Strong arms, muscled chest with just the right amount of silky blond hair, shaped like an inverted triangle that dipped into those jeans riding low on his hips.

And then she saw his face. Eyes a deep blue the sky would be jealous of. A strong chin. Those dimples. His blond hair, mussed by the fall breeze and the effort of his work, only added to his sex appeal.

Don't go there, the little voice warned.

"Mind your own business, little voice," she murmured, trying hard not to be the voyeur. She wasn't succeeding. She watched, afraid to put a name to the feeling that coursed through her. The sawing stopped suddenly, jarring Zoe back to reality. She stepped back from the screen a few feet, keeping her presence hidden but locking her gaze on Ryan.

Muscles she hadn't known he had rippled as he worked. Wearing work gloves, he bundled the cut branches with rope and in two trips to the back of the house he had the side yard cleared.

She opened the screen door, and leaned out just far enough to watch as he stored the saw in the shed and returned carrying a ladder and pruning sheers. She quickly shut the door as he passed by and into the front yard.

What was he up to now? Her curiosity piqued

about why Ryan was doing yard work at his child-hood home, Zoe quietly slid out the door and crept along a few feet behind Ryan. He slipped the shears into his back pocket, positioned the ladder against the rose-covered trellis and started to climb.

Her eyes widened as she took in the complete pic-ture, including the For Sale sign the real estate agent had pounded into the lawn less than a week ago, which now sported the word Sold across its face.

Once Ryan saw the Sold sign posted in the front yard of the house, he felt the pride that went along with ownership.

And, he admitted, a little bit of the terror.

He'd been fortunate the owners had moved out once the purchase contract had been signed, and that they'd agreed to allow him to do some renovations inside before the title transferred.

There was no rush to trim the trees and bushes and prune the roses. The yard work could have waited until the weekend, but Ryan had returned from two days in Philadelphia with a mission. Two missions, actually. Turn the house into a home. And deal with Zoe. He had all the time in the world to complete the former, less than two weeks to accomplish the latter, what he cryptically called *Mission: Impossible*.

He bundled the cut branches from the oak tree and carried them to the area of the backyard where he'd decided to store firewood. Although cool weather still was weeks away, it never hurt to be prepared.

He frowned, thinking of how unprepared he'd been to deal with Zoe since the moment he'd seen her handcuffed and in jail; how he'd followed her from shop to shop Saturday afternoon, not concerned about whether or not he was making a nuisance of himself. He had been determined to discover what it was about Zoe Russell that so intrigued him. That was all. He had no intention of getting involved with her romantically.

If he could just figure out what it was about her that kept her popping into his thoughts, Ryan knew he could work out a solution to the problem. He just hadn't counted on Philadelphia getting in the way.

It was bad enough he had to deal with the continuing nightmares, now he had to deal with the Internal Affairs office of the Philadelphia Police Department. More questions he didn't have answers to. They wanted to close the case. He had argued Sean was more than a case.

The nightmares were bad enough, the worst was having to relive the night Sean died in front of a team of officers who kept their expressions stony and their opinions to themselves. But during endless questioning over the past two days, he'd felt tried and convicted for not having done the right thing. For not saving Sean. Each time he retold the story, Ryan felt himself die a little, as well.

He knew all the questioning was part of the drill, that eventually he'd be exonerated of any wrongdoing, but Ryan still felt guilty as hell.

As if there wasn't enough guilt piling up in his little corner of the world, he was still reeling from the shock of discovering he'd like to have Zoe Russell stripped, naked and underneath him in his bed every night for the next week if he thought he wouldn't roast in hell afterward.

He could only hope he didn't see her today. No telling what he'd do. Kiss her. Throttle her. The possibilities were endless.

He looked up at the trellis, overgrown with roses, and tried to think back to the time when his parents were alive and his mother had directed his father on every cut and trim to keep the roses healthy and in continual bloom. He'd been happy then, unconcerned about the future.

Not true now. Both his personal and professional life was in turmoil. Keeping Zoe at arm's length because it was the smart, the rational, the fair thing to do, was becoming more and more difficult because Ryan knew instinctively that she was the one person who could help him see the forest for all the trees. Or the beauty of the roses among the mess of brambles and bushes.

Ryan climbed the ladder, reached into his back pocket for the pruning shears and started pinching back the blossoms that had withered, and cutting back the vines that had tangled with the trellis.

"Ouch!"

He heard Zoe's cry, looked down, mildly irritated to see her standing below, a few thorns caught in her curly red hair, the rest of the cut vegetation at her feet. She was dressed in white shorts and a bright green T-shirt that matched her eyes. The amused look on her heart-shaped face as she picked the thorns from her hair stirred his blood.

His heart beat a tattoo. What was it about her that

made him feel protective, exasperated and sexually stirred up all at once? No answer came readily to mind.

He climbed down the ladder and pulled on a blue T-shirt. He walked over to her and without asking permission, carefully removed the remaining bits of thorn from her hair. She reached up and caught his wrist. Their gazes locked. Thinking about kissing Zoe was one thing. Kissing Zoe was another.

Her eyes filled with a confusion he could sympathize with. He broke away and walked over to the steps leading up to the front porch. Leaning against one of the pillars, he watched her warily as he pulled a cigar from his front pocket. His hand shook as he lit it, and he was aware by the smile in her eyes that she'd seen his hand shake. She rattled him. And he wasn't happy that she could. "It'll take some time, but I'll get the gardens back in shape again."

"Does police work in Riverbend pay so little you need to moonlight?"

He just shrugged.

"The family who lived here recently moved to Cleveland." Zoe slowly walked toward him. "The sign says Sold. Wonder who'll be moving in." She paused, looked at him directly. "Those things will kill you."

"Just one of my better vices." Ryan inhaled the rich aroma, and blew smoke circles into the air. "That new owner is me."

He saw he'd surprised her. And for some ridiculous reason that pleased him.

"I thought your time in Riverbend was…was…"

She seemed to struggle with the words. Probably looking for the proper one to put him in his proper place. And that pleased him, too, knowing that no matter her mood, the Zoe Russell he remembered could turn on feisty with the best of them. He was glad to know that hadn't changed because he'd always appreciated that about her.

"Try temporary," he offered dryly, and blew another cycle of smoke rings, expecting it to get a rise out of her and surprised when it did not. "I'm going back to Philly...soon. But when I saw the For Sale sign, something inside me snapped. I'd let the house go once in anger after my parents died. I couldn't let it go to someone else this time. So, for as long as I'm living here, I'm living *here*."

She looked a little tired, a little too pale. He had the urge to help her, to comfort her. But he'd bet he was the last person on earth from whom Zoe Russell would accept any kind of comfort.

"Another day, another day of work," she said a little too brightly.

"One of those big-drama days," he drawled.

"Lately they've all been big-drama days," she muttered, but his sharp ears caught her words, tinged with sadness that he thought bordered on bitterness.

"I thought you loved your job."

"I do," she said quickly. "Most days," she amended. "Some mornings as I'm fighting my way into the subways, I think about what my life would have been like if I'd stayed in Riverbend, married Jake—like I threatened to do—and raised little tadpoles.

"Don't you remember?" She moved to stand in front of him and poked at his chest. "The day after Jake shoved a tadpole down my bathing suit, I climbed back into the fishpond and collected two tadpoles. And told everyone they were my new family and I was going to watch them create little tadpoles."

She started to giggle, and within seconds the giggles turned into hiccups of laughter. She bonelessly dropped toward the stoop, whooping like a crane.

He snaked his arm around her shoulder just long enough to keep her from sliding off the stoop and into the freshly mowed grass. "And you told me they were boy tadpoles, and they'd grow into toads. And Kate said if I kissed a toad I'd turn him into my Prince Charming and..." She paused, drew herself up. The smile was gone from her face. "What a silly thing to remember."

"Not so silly," he said softly.

A few minutes ago he'd fought the urge to kiss her. He doubted she had any idea of the power she held. With a look she could make his blood stir, make him want...

Make him want *her*. He burned for her—hot and quick. Images of them together, in bed, naked and touching each other all over, blurred in his mind. Unless he let go of her right now, he was going to kiss her senseless. And maybe more. That would be the biggest mistake of this big-drama day.

There was all that unfinished business in Philadelphia. He had nothing inside to offer a woman, any woman, especially a woman like Zoe, who deserved a man who could commit totally. He'd lost too many people who mattered to him—his parents, his partner—that he wasn't about to risk his heart again. He wanted Zoe, but no way would he take her, knowing that at any moment fate could intervene and she could disappear with the wind.

"I can't remember the last time I laughed like that." She stood, let out a deep breath and relaxed against the railing. "So out of control."

"Nothing wrong with that," Ryan sad, "as long as you keep control of the out of control."

She laughed, as he'd meant her to. "That felt good. I was really looking forward to these two weeks. Coming home. Spending time with Kate and Mom."

Ryan relaxed. She was here for now. Then she'd be heading back to the Big Apple. With relief, Ryan felt that moment of craziness, when he'd been burning to kiss her, to indulge himself in mindless sex with her, pass.

Zoe drew in a breath and as she exhaled she ordered herself to relax. There'd been all this static electricity snapping between them, a kind of sexual tension she'd come to expect whenever she and Ryan were together.

She pushed all thoughts of indulging herself, flirting with Ryan, making him see her for the woman she was, out of her mind. She was worried she was getting in way over her head. And that she'd be dealing with a bruised heart before she left Riverbend.

She forced her eyes to wander up and down the street that she used to call home.

Not much had changed. But everything had changed. The houses up and down the block were older. Some were shabbier. Others boasted new siding or paint jobs. The trees seemed larger, taller. There were new neighbors living across the street. And Penelope's best friend, recently widowed, had sold her house on the other side of Kate's to a young couple with a two-year-old toddler and a baby girl.

She was no longer eighteen, no longer naive or idealistic. No matter how much she wanted to turn back the clock ten years, she couldn't. She could, however, move ahead, and deal with her conflicted feelings about Ryan. That was the responsible, adult action to take. And in less than two weeks, she'd be back in Manhattan. Back at *Wake Up, America*, back to the life that was hers, the life she'd always dreamed about.

It wasn't Ryan who scared her. It was the intense feelings she carried inside that worried her. Flirting with him to teach him a lesson was one thing. But she couldn't, she wouldn't, let him sneak back into her life and try to disrupt what she'd accomplished, both personally and professionally, during the past ten years.

Because if she did, and if they started to rebuild their friendship, or if that friendship developed into something more, she didn't think she could survive when he left again. Not if. But when. Even if he had bought his old family house. Even if he spent an afternoon cutting down dead tree branches and pruning rose bushes.

She'd learned to live without him once. She couldn't bear having to do so again.

Because she couldn't imagine the Ryan O'Connor

standing in front of her, the man who thrived on dangerous police work, would ever be happy settling down forever in Riverbend. Not that she had plans to settle here forever, either.

The words spilled out of her mouth before she could pull them back. "Can I ask you a personal question? It's not about why you left Philadelphia. I'd like to know, but I expect you'll tell me when you're ready. It's why come back to Riverbend?"

He took his time answering. "It was number one on a short list of options."

She waited for him to go on. When he didn't, she said with false brightness, "Thank you for clearing up my confusion."

"You're welcome." The tone of his voice didn't match the cordiality of his words. "How about a glass of your mother's iced tea?"

He headed across the yard, opened the side screen door to Kate's house and disappeared into the kitchen, leaving Zoe no choice but to follow.

Except he wasn't in the kitchen. She found him in the living room watching the tape of her entertainment special. He held the remote, fast-forwarded for a few seconds, then played the tape. She watched him as he watched the TV screen attentively and then turned to her with a startled expression on his face. "This is good."

"I'm still tinkering. It's not finished," Zoe said, hating the shade of defensiveness she heard in her voice. And hating that she felt she had to explain herself to Ryan.

"Don't put yourself down," Ryan admonished her.

"You enjoy your work. You're being paid, and pretty well I hear, to do something you love. Not everyone's as lucky."

"I'm not doing it for the money," she replied. "Or for the fame."

"I never said you were."

"Producing a TV show isn't easy. I've spent..." She stopped in midsentence and watched as he walked over to the fireplace and peered at the clock sitting on the mantle. "What are you doing?"

"Just checking to see how many minutes we've gone without arguing about something."

She locked her gaze on him. He wasn't laughing. He stared just as intently at her. Zoe thought she saw a flicker of a smile on his face, but then it was gone.

"The iced tea?" he reminded her gently.

Zoe hurried into the kitchen, anxious to fix him the tea, even more anxious to get him out of the house. She grabbed a clean glass from the dishwasher, tossed a few ice cubes into it and poured the tea.

She felt pressure on her shoulders, stepped back abruptly, let out a whoosh of air as her back hit his chest, her heel his toe. She turned, thrust the glass of tea at him.

Ryan stood so close they practically touched. And then she noticed his blue T-shirt, liberally sprinkled with big drops of iced tea. Their eyes connected. He was remembering the soapsuds incident, too. She traced one of the spots with her fingertip and felt the sizzle. She looked into Ryan's face and saw the same mix of desire and confusion she felt.

"Zoe." Ryan's voice broke. He stroked her cheek,

and warmth rushed through her body and soul like a wild fire.

Touch me again, her eyes implored him. With his fingertips Ryan gently traced her features, her eyes, the cheekbones, the fullness of her lips, then he skimmed down the curve of her neck, and cupped her chin.

Ryan ignored his wet T-shirt and instead concentrated on Zoe. He could shout out thousands of reasons not to kiss her. But only one reason to do so, because once upon a time he'd cared deeply for her. And no matter what the future held for him, if only one thing was clear to him, he needed to mend their broken relationship so the healing could begin in his heart and soul.

He'd lost Sean, his parents and too many other friends over the past decade to risk losing more. He'd lost Zoe, too, but fate had intervened. He had a second chance, if he was willing to take it.

He traced her facial features, committing each one to memory. And smiled when she did the same, at first timidly, then more boldly. Suddenly impatient, Ryan drew her to him.

Zoe's eyes fluttered closed and she waited for him to kiss her. Up popped the memory of their first kiss, when she was sixteen. That kiss was supposed to seal a lifelong friendship that had splintered two years later. What would a shared kiss today mean to him? A kiss of friendship, or a lover's kiss, one that smoldered and promised more? Zoe shivered at the thought.

And then she felt Ryan's lips brushing gently on

hers. The tip of his tongue traced the shape of her lips. His hand at the small of her back pressed her closer, so she could feel and hear the frantic beat of his heart. As frantic as hers.

All rational thought left her as Ryan—finally!—deepened the kiss and the lazy sizzle turned into a jarring jolt. And just as abruptly he ended it.

Zoe opened her eyes to see him watching her warily. "It was just a kiss," she said softly.

"Just a kiss," he agreed.

Then he drew her to him and kissed her again.

Chapter Five

This kiss smoldered like a forest fire ready to flare. Zoe might have pulled away from the unexpected but oh-so-pleasurable heat if she hadn't felt Ryan's hands on the small of her back, gently holding her close, just like before. So she leaned into the kiss, and with the tip of her tongue slowly traced the shape of his lips. Just like he'd done before.

The warmth spread, heating her blood so she could almost feel the molecules rush through her body. She wanted something more…something she couldn't quite name or define. But whatever *it* was, she knew it had to be something vital to her being.

A promise only Ryan could fulfill. All rational thought fled. It was as though she'd been waiting for *this* kiss all her life.

"I need to touch you," Ryan said. He pressed her closer, so close that she felt the heat and hardness of his body. His hands moved upward, tracing her spine, cupping the back of her neck, her chin and then gently touching the swell of her breast.

She sighed, closed her eyes as she placed her hand atop the one he held to her breast. For a moment she could feel her heart beat beneath their hands. When she pressed her hand against his chest he slowly backed away. She opened her eyes to see the startled look in his.

She'd heard no bells. No whistles. No marching band. No hallelujah choir joyfully singing "he's still the one." Yet the words played through her mind and she smiled to herself.

Zoe kept her gaze on his, wondering what he'd do next, what he might say. Or might not say. Only when Ryan finally smiled, a smile bracketed by those killer dimples, did she let herself partially relax, until he ran a finger playfully down her forehead to the tip of her nose.

Then, only sheer will—and the countertop behind her—kept Zoe from melting into a puddle at Ryan's feet.

"What's happening here?" she asked breathlessly, trying hard not to let him see how his touch, or those damn dimples, affected her equilibrium.

Ryan didn't answer. He just kissed her again.

Zoe hated to be idle, so Friday morning found her up in the attic with a personal mission to clear out all the stuff of her childhood that had remained behind when she'd left Riverbend six years ago. Kate, to her credit, had carefully stored Zoe's possessions in marked boxes and placed them in a corner of the cramped space.

She drew a small footstool up near the window and started on the first box, grateful Kate had merely folded the cardboard flaps rather than taped the boxes shut. She could hear her sister downstairs speaking on the telephone, Kate's voice unusually sharp with whoever was on the other end of the line.

She gazed out the window to the street below. Kate's smart red convertible, a wedding gift from her fiancé, sat parked in the driveway, the back seat packed with engagement presents that Kate wanted returned or exchanged at several of Cincinnati's pricey department stores.

As much as Zoe hated being indoors on such a beautiful fall morning, she'd rather be here plowing into her past than stuck shopping with Kate for the next few hours, facing any number of sales clerks assigned to their store's bridal departments.

Or remembering Ryan's kisses.

Instead, she thought about her network special, finally edited and ready to be broadcast the following Friday night. She considered the promo she'd film early next week, plugging the program, and wondered how it would feel to answer questions rather than ask them.

Her thoughts again slid back to Ryan. She'd seen him several times since Tuesday, when her world—and her view of Ryan's place in it—had tilted and not quite righted itself again. They'd spoken casually, no mention of the kisses and heat that had flared between them. No mention of them seeing each other again, other than at the upcoming rehearsal dinner, and, of course, the wedding.

Zoe forced herself to dig into the box, where she discovered little of interest. A doll, a small embroidered box filled with crayons and makeup, a dried and pressed corsage, probably from a high school dance.

"My diary." That she remembered. She jiggled the lock until it gave way and opened. She skimmed over the first pages, written when she was barely sixteen. She came across the entry where she'd scribbled her feelings about Ryan's first kiss.

"He kissed me," she read aloud. "On the forehead! Then his lips slipped, and touched mine. Goose bumps ran up and down my arms. His lips felt like rubber…not at all like what I'd read in romance novels…"

"I don't remember writing that." But there was nothing rubbery about the way the adult Ryan kissed now. Those kisses had made her hot, made her sizzle and left her wanting more. She shook her head to clear it. She couldn't let it happen again.

Why not? asked the little voice. *You liked it. He liked it. You're both unattached, healthy adults. What's wrong with living for the minute?*

"Because those minutes add up and end up costing plenty," Zoe murmured as she continued reading the diary. She skimmed the next several pages, stopping when she came to the entry she'd written several days before her high school graduation. The entry was in bold, angry lettering,

DADDY AND MOM ARE FIGHTING AGAIN.
IT'S NEVER BEEN THIS BAD. MOM'S IN
TEARS. KATE'S CRYING, TOO. I'M TRY-
ING TO BE BRAVE BUT IT'S NOT WORK-
ING. I HAVEN'T SEEN RYAN IN DAYS.
THERE'S NO ONE TO TALK TO. I FEEL SO
ALONE.

"I feel so alone," Zoe whispered, repeating the
words she'd just read. She'd been emotionally adrift
those days following the announcement of her parents' separation, her father moving out and the dis-
covery that Ryan and Kate had eloped. There had
been no one she could talk to, no one to share in her
grief, because the one person she'd counted on to be
there for her, had been gone, as well.

"Zoe," Kate called out, her voice drifting up the
stairs. "I need to talk to you."

"I'm up in the attic." Hearing the rapid tap-tap of
her sister's footsteps, Zoe closed the diary and tossed
it back into the box seconds before Kate appeared in
the doorway.

"There's a problem at the store." Kate idly
glanced around and absently brushed a cobweb from
her hair. "What are you doing up here?" Before Zoe
could answer, she barreled on. "I can't go to Cincinnati today."

Zoe's heart leaped in joy. No mall trip! "That's
too bad…"

"You'll take back the gifts for me, won't you?"
Kate dangled the key to her new sports car right in
front of Zoe.

Maybe a long, fast ride to Cincinnati in a snazzy red convertible would drive out of her mind the painful words she'd written in the diary. Words that ten years later still had the power to hurt her.

"Bet I can con Mom into helping." Zoe snagged the key and pocketed it before Kate could change her mind. "And pump her about her mysterious friend."

Kate laughed. "Whoever he is, he's the best-kept secret in Southern Ohio. So, what's going on between you and Ryan? And don't say *nothing*. I've seen the way the two of you look at each other when you think no one's watching."

"You've been throwing him at me since the moment I arrived home. I know I warned you about matchmaking. Ryan told me he had words with you, as well."

"He did. I didn't listen. Is it working?" Kate pulled up another footstool and sat. "C'mon, tell me. We've always shared our secrets."

Kate smiled mischievously and Zoe, who vividly recalled one secret *not* shared—the night Kate and Ryan eloped—wanted to wipe the silly grin off her sister's face.

"We kissed. The end. And that's all there is to it. Some secrets," Zoe stood and said in a prim tone of voice guaranteed to make Kate laugh, "you're better off not knowing."

And was gratified when her sister chuckled. Some secrets, Zoe thought as she followed Kate down the stairs, weren't meant for sharing with a sister once married, no matter how briefly, to a man who, with a mere kiss, could make Zoe melt.

* * *

Zoe dressed quickly, anxious to get on the road and eager to put some real distance between her and Ryan. She punched out her mother's phone number and frowned when she got the voice mail.

"Mom, it's Zoe. I'm coming to Cincy today. Thought we could have lunch. Talk. My treat. Catch up with you later."

She couldn't keep whatever was smoldering between her and Ryan a secret from Kate—or her mother—forever. Give Kate an inch, and her romantic sister would have Zoe and Ryan walking down the aisle—not as maid of honor and best man, but as bride and groom.

Give her mother *half* an inch, and Penelope would scour the baby books searching for names for her first grandchild.

Anyway, Zoe thought as she reached into her jewelry box for her emerald earrings, maybe she and her mother could trade contemporary dating secrets. Although Penelope hadn't said another word about her male friend.

Zoe held up the emeralds, a gift to herself when she'd gotten the promotion at *Wake Up*. Sinfully expensive, they were a symbol of her success. But for some reason wearing them today didn't feel right. She placed them back in the jewelry box, and took out simple silver hoops instead.

As she fitted the earrings, she checked her appearance in the full-length mirror hanging on the closet door. And laughed. With her red hair, the nut-brown slacks and sage sweater, she almost matched the colors of the leaves on her oak tree.

The oak tree made her think of Ryan, again. Everything familiar in Riverbend made her think of him. Of what they'd once meant to each other. Of a friendship that seemed so remote days ago, appeared... possible now. Or maybe more than a friendship, if she was willing to take a chance. If she was willing to trust Ryan. More important, if she could trust herself.

Zoe took a good long look at herself in the mirror. She was twenty-eight, single, reasonably attractive, living in the city of her dreams, right at the beginning of what looked to be a brilliant career and...and, she frowned. She stared long and hard at her reflection in the mirror. She'd wished, and her dreams had come true.

''You're supposed to be happy, damn it,'' she told her reflection. Except Zoe wasn't. She couldn't pinpoint the reason why. Or the moment she discovered that being independent wasn't much fun when you were alone.

''Why can't I find what Kate has with Alec. Or meet someone like Mom's mysterious stranger?''

Instead, she had her little voice scolding her to ''keep away from Ryan O'Connor. He hurt you once. Don't give him a chance to hurt you again.'' Zoe had tried to keep her distance. But the man just seemed to be everywhere she went. And when he wasn't there, he was inside her head. And while in her head she knew it was past time she dealt with all her confused and unresolved feelings about Ryan, her fragile heart wasn't ready.

She spun away from the mirror, grabbed her purse and started down the stairs. And jerked to a stop when she saw Ryan leaning against the railing at the bottom step. He was dressed in faded jeans and a T-shirt, a weathered brown leather bomber jacket tossed over his shoulder.

His blond hair was mussed, the smile on his face welcoming. An all-too-sexy package ready, waiting and willing to be unwrapped. The part of her that wanted to kiss him senseless was busy waging war with the part of her not in any mood to deal with him.

She arched a brow. "No criminals to catch today?"

His smile broadened. "Night shift."

"That doesn't explain why you're here."

He jogged up the steps. "Let's go."

"I'm going to Cincinnati. You can go to…" Her pointed look told him exactly where he could go.

"I'm your chauffeur. He shrugged. "Hey, I know you can drive yourself, but when Kate called…" His voice trailed off. "Look," he said, a bit more forcefully, "I thought it would give us a chance to talk more about getting our friendship back on track." He paused. "And the kisses. We need to talk about them, too."

While she couldn't believe Kate had thrown them together again, she knew Ryan was right. She'd spent the entire morning, no the entire past week, weighing and analyzing her thoughts concerning him. She'd found no clear-cut answers, just a vague longing for what they used to have together. That wasn't enough to make her radically change her life. Or radically change her opinion of him.

They may have shared bone-shattering, mind-blowing kisses, but that didn't mean Ryan's feelings about getting emotionally involved with her had changed. Still, she couldn't believe the man who had kissed her with so much pent-up longing didn't have strong feelings for her.

If nothing else, she owed it to Ryan—and to herself—to see if they could really be friends once again. And maybe in the future, something more.

With a promise to herself that she'd be the one driving home, she tossed him Kate's car key. "You carry the heavy packages and you buy lunch."

Ryan knew that he had been the one to point out that they needed to talk, but now he was at a loss at how to start, so the first half of the forty-minute drive to Cincinnati was spent in silence.

Obviously uncomfortable, Zoe began pressing the radio buttons in search of the local jazz station, but the radio wasn't cooperating. All she could find was loud rock and static.

With a sigh, Ryan brushed Zoe's hands away from the buttons and shut off the radio. For the past several days, he'd been searching for a way to get her alone so they could talk. Kate's telephone call inviting him to accompany Zoe to Cincinnati had been the excuse he'd been waiting for.

But now that he had Zoe in the car, at sixty miles per hour on a busy highway, he wasn't quite sure what to say. Sometimes, he thought wryly, winging it was the best way to put suspects at ease. The tactic could work with her. "Ever thought much about what you'll be doing five years from now?"

She leaned against the headrest and rolled her eyes. "Ace detective that you are, I'm sure you'll eventually get to the part relevant to Kate and Alec's wedding."

He decided to ignore her sarcasm. "Or what you might regret?"

"I'm not going another round of Truth or Dare."

"Will you listen to what I have to say?" At her curt nod, he made a decision to tell her everything, even if this wasn't the best time, or best place. He took a deep breath, slowly exhaled and continued. "About six months ago, my partner on the force… Sean…he died."

She turned to glance at him. "Ryan, I'm so sorry."

"He was my best friend. We were like brothers. And he was probably the only person, since you, that I let myself get really close to." He paused for her response.

"Will you tell me what happened?"

"He was murdered." Ryan felt the pain as though it was fresh. "It was my fault."

"I can't believe that."

"I didn't pull the trigger, but all the same, I let him down." Ryan gripped the steering wheel tightly and locked his gaze on the road ahead. Relief poured through him. Zoe still understood him well enough not to offer pity or silly platitudes—both were guaranteed to stir more anger and despair in him.

He eased off the highway and by the time he'd

parked the car near the mall entrance, he'd told her about the drug sting they'd been working on. About Sean's penchant for fast food and faster women. Of missing Sean's phone call.

He kept his tone flat, his words spare, his gaze locked on her face. "We were off duty. I'd gone over to the local cop hangout, expecting to see Sean. Thought we might shoot a few rounds of pool. He wasn't there. I started flirting with the barmaid. Just flirting," he added hastily. "She'd been dating Sean the past month. It seemed to be going good.

"It wasn't until a few beers later that I realized my pager had gone off. His message was brief. To the point. Action was going down. He couldn't wait. It was after midnight before I'd tracked him down. Into one of the worst areas of Philly. Sean and some other guy stood at the far end of a dimly lit alley. Arguing loudly. I couldn't make out what they were saying." Ryan paused, tried to keep his thoughts focused.

"I'd taken maybe two steps when I felt something like fire in my side. I must have shouted Sean's name, because he turned, shouted at me to go back, and ran toward me. A minute later he was down, with one in the back. He couldn't move."

Zoe squeezed his hand and he squeezed hers back. "You were shot, too?"

"Barely nicked. Hurt like hell." He hadn't realized how free he felt in telling Zoe, knowing she would listen and not judge. "I had no idea what happened to the guy who hit me."

He swallowed. This was the hard part. He turned away so he wouldn't have to see her reaction. Or have her see the tears welling in his eyes. ''I got the dirtbag who shot Sean. I got him good. But not before he stood over Sean and fired again.'' His voice broke. ''And again.''

''I understand why you blame yourself,'' Zoe said softly. She cupped his chin and turned his face toward hers. ''But it wasn't your fault. Sean made a choice. He took a risk, and risked your life, as well.''

Ryan broke contact and scrubbed his hands down his face. ''If you'd asked me before six months ago, what I thought I'd be doing five years from now, I'd have told you, still playing pool with my best friend Sean, still flirting with his girlfriends and still wearing a cop badge in Philly.''

''Regrets?'' Zoe thought back to what he'd asked her at the beginning of their conversation. She could see that the months since Sean's death had left more than an emotional toll on Ryan. His face was lean, the lines under his eyes pronounced. And she understood by the tone of his voice, and his body language, he'd found it difficult to tell her what had happened.

''Too many to list. Not being there in time to save Sean.'' Zoe's pulse jumped when he took her hand, kissed her palm and placed her hand over his heart. ''Not being there for you back then.''

She touched her forehead to his. And understood the effect of what he'd gone through. He was battling guilt, and it appeared as though guilt was winning. ''I'm glad you told me about Sean.''

''There's more.'' He paused, scrubbed his hands down his face again. ''I shouldn't have kissed you.''

"Why?" Zoe asked carefully. "Why shouldn't you have kissed me?"

"Because I want our friendship back again," he said patiently. "Just the way it was. Our friendship was...is...important to me."

"Even friendships grow and change. Nothing in life stays the same." She sighed. Just when she thought they were making progress he tosses this nonsense at her.

"Zoe," he groaned, "I'm trying to be noble here."

"Stuff the nobility, Ryan. How about being honest with me? Or, more importantly, honest with yourself."

Zoe had wanted to move forward with Ryan, to get rid of the clutter of their past. But right now what she really wanted was to punch him hard in the gut. Instead, she reached into the back seat for the packages and thrust them into his hands.

"I thought married couples waited until after the wedding to return unwanted gifts," Ryan groused good-naturedly as he stepped onto the up escalator leading to the bridal department.

Zoe felt sorry for what Ryan had gone through, first with his parents dying in the car accident, and then Sean's murder in the line of duty. But what bothered her now was the ease with which Ryan could turn his emotions on and off to suit his moods.

He wanted her. He didn't want her. He kissed her. But he shouldn't have kissed her. Here was yet another reminder how much he'd changed in the past decade, and how much she still didn't know about him.

For now, she'd follow his lead and pretend there was nothing going on between them other than rebuilding their friendship.

"Kate and Alec are blending their homes and I guess they pretty much have everything. I'm sure they don't need another toaster oven or—" she looked at the last gift to be returned "—another silver coffeepot. But what about couples beginning a life together? Or those who've married, now are divorced or widowed and are tying the knot again? It'd be fun to find out what goes in those trousseaus. And it would make a great piece for *Wake Up*."

She looked up to find Ryan staring at her in wonder. "Don't you ever quit working?"

"Not if I want to stay in the game," Zoe replied automatically.

"That's important to you." Ryan framed his words as a statement, but Zoe heard the question.

"For now it is," she said.

Zoe stepped into a bridal department steeped in chaos. At the far end of the room, two sleekly dressed women expertly stapled silver and white bunting across a makeshift stage, while another woman unsuccessfully tried to coax a microphone to life.

At one side of the stage, tables had been set up to hold computers that likely contained the names, wedding dates and gift preferences of the area's brides-to-be. Other workers stacked promotional flyers.

Zoe grabbed Ryan's sleeve and dragged him to the side. She planted herself against a wall, and a quick survey of the room told her everything she needed to know.

"What's going on?" Ryan asked. His gaze held a look of confusion, like a fish out of water, one just hooked and unsure of what might happen next.

"It's a bridal show," she whispered, pointing to the women—all ages, all shapes and all sizes—filling the rows of steel-back chairs. "You're the only man here with all those sexy-looking models—" she wagged a finger toward the break in the curtain "—strutting their stuff wearing nothing more than lace teddies and satin robes revealing more than they conceal."

"I'm outta here." He raised his hands in surrender and slowly backed away. "I'll give you ten minutes, then meet me down in the coffee shop near the bookstore."

"Coward," Zoe called after him.

Ryan stopped in his tracks, a defiant look in his eye as he purposefully strode back to her side. He leaned back against the wall, his arms negligently crossed in front of his chest. "Before the day's over, you'll eat those words."

"There's a good story here," she said, "just waiting for someone to tell it."

"Time to take your seats," said a harried salesclerk wearing a nametag shaped like a wedding bell and identifying her as Vera. She pressed by Zoe and flounced up the two steps onto the runway that jutted out from the center. Vera smartly snapped two opaque curtain panels into place before gently easing the women in front of the microphone off the stage.

Vera tapped the mike several times with the tip of her perfectly manicured nails. The resulting screech had Zoe covering her ears. "Quiet now. We're almost ready to begin."

Zoe stepped back to the far edge of the room, trying to take it all in, imagining how the scene would look on tape. She bumped into a younger version of Vera.

"You don't have a gift bag," the younger Vera said in dismay. "Or a raffle ticket. That won't do." She thrust a bag and a shiny silver card into Zoe's hands before disappearing behind the stage.

Zoe had to admit that despite the older Vera's severe looks and style, the woman knew how to work a crowd. For the next fifteen minutes, Vera described the clothes with words that made Zoe's mouth water with desire. The audience responded, as well, clapping when the models walked through the curtain, and again when they strolled down the runway.

Vera stepped up to the mike. "And now, the last of our special raffles. We're one of only four stores in the entire country to offer this prize." She dug into a wicker basket overflowing with tickets. "Number B3628, come claim an all-expenses paid trip to New York City where the staff of *Wake Up, America* will help you plan a wedding to remember!"

There were a few murmurs from the crowd, but no one stepped forward to grab the prize.

"That's you," shrieked the younger Vera, who'd appeared next to Zoe out of nowhere. She grabbed the ticket and waved it wildly in the older Vera's direction.

Zoe paled as all eyes fixed on her.

Chapter Six

Ryan immediately tuned into Zoe's distress. She hadn't moved a muscle and had that deer-caught-in-the-headlights look that he'd seen countless times on the faces of crime victims.

"What a mess," she whispered. "How am I going to explain this at *Wake Up*?" She squared her shoulders, forced a smile and sighed when Vera didn't smile back.

Ryan grabbed the ticket from the younger woman who was staring at Zoe in dismay and jogged up to the stage. He knew she wouldn't appreciate his interference, but it was in his nature to take charge. Besides, the silence in the room had grown uncomfortable. "Excuse us a minute, folks," he said into the mike. He drew Vera aside.

"Do you know who that woman is?" He pointed to Zoe, who looked back at him quizzically.

"Not our winner?" Vera's face and voice frowned in unison.

"That's Zoe Russell, from *Wake Up, America.*" He paused, waited for the information to sink in. "Understand?"

"Definitely not our winner," Vera said.

"Zoe's visiting family in the area," Ryan murmured conspiratorially, "but I bet she'd come up here and help you select the real winner."

Vera stepped over to the mike, apologizing to the audience about the slight delay. She then conferred with an assistant. When she turned back to Ryan, she nodded briefly.

Ryan left the stage. He swung an arm comfortably over Zoe's shoulder. And was gratified when she sank into his side.

He tried not to think about how right it felt to have her there. He felt no regrets about spilling out his story, or his feelings, about the night Sean died. No matter how much Zoe tempted him, he knew not diving into a romantic relationship with her was best for both of them. If he could regain just a little of the ground he'd lost with her ten years ago, he'd have accomplished something he could be proud of.

He'd trusted his instincts, and they'd told him to trust her. He wished she trusted him. Still, whether she realized it or not, whether she trusted him or not, she needed his help. "You know what you have to do?"

"Start sending out résumés?" she joked. "I can imagine tomorrow's tabloid headline, Zoe Wakes Up

To Show's Top Prize. The suits in New York will never understand.''

''They will if you turn this into something positive.'' He gently maneuvered her toward the stage. ''Go on up there. Act like this was part of the plan.''

She strode up to Vera, exchanged a few words that seemed to reassure, and then turned toward the audience with a huge smile filling her face.

How could she have forgotten about *Wake Up*'s nationwide fall bridal promotion? She'd chalk the memory loss up to the pressures she'd be under trying to get her entertainment special edited, planning Kate's wedding and, of course, Ryan's return into her life.

Zoe took a deep breath and prayed she could avoid what could turn out to be an enormous PR disaster for *Wake Up, America.* She hadn't needed Ryan's help, but she was smart enough that she appreciated it. They'd been a team so many years ago that she'd forgotten, no, she'd forced herself to forget, how important his support had been. She sneaked a glance in Ryan's direction. He smiled, gave her a thumbs-up.

She smiled back and began to speak. ''Hi, I'm Zoe Russell. I hope you recognize me from *Wake Up, America.*''

There was a slight smattering of applause. So far, so good, she thought, her confidence gaining. Ryan was right. She had just enough lemons to make a pitcher of lemonade, one large enough to satisfy this audience. ''You watch *Wake Up*?'' she asked a twenty-something blonde in the front row who wore a sparkling diamond ring that looked to weigh carets.

"That's great," she said when the young woman nodded her reply.

"I guess somebody thought it would be funny for me, who's made being single her career, to win a wedding of a lifetime."

She paused at the smattering of applause, then glanced in Ryan's direction, not quite sure what to make of the thoughtful look on his face. "Actually, my sister's getting married next week. I'm her maid of honor. Third time this year I've found myself walking a few steps ahead of the bride."

Stronger applause followed, along with some laughter. Zoe beckoned Vera forward. "I'm thrilled to represent *Wake Up, America*, and hope you'll continue tuning us in every morning." She reached into the basket Vera held and picked out a ticket. "And the winner of a wedding to remember, courtesy of *Wake Up, America*, is…C56017."

A young woman from the back shouted out, "That's me!" With three other women trailing behind her—likely her bridesmaids—she made her way to the stage. Zoe graciously endured another five minutes of hugging, kissing and screaming before she could offer her congratulations and a promise to see the bride-to-be when she came to Manhattan.

Zoe hurried off the stage, praying that if there were any amateur videographers in the audience they only caught the last half of her performance on tape or, even better, forgot to load their cameras.

"That's not an event I'll ever forget. Or want to repeat." She waited for Ryan to unlock the passenger car door, then kissed his cheek before sliding into the seat. "Thanks for saving the day. If you hadn't been there, I'd have dashed down the escalator and out the store screaming madly."

"With Vera and the video cam man right behind you," Ryan said as he took his place behind the driver's seat.

Zoe settled in the car and adjusted her seat belt. "I'm not used to someone stepping in and helping me." She chose her next words carefully. "I liked that we were working as a team."

Ryan braked suddenly. "Say that again."

"It's easy," Zoe said slowly, "to admire a man who knows exactly what to do, takes charge so effortlessly and brings about a happy ending."

"A compliment?" He grinned, eased the car onto the highway. "Now you admire me. Does that mean you're buying lunch?"

His grin was infectious, the fall day too beautiful, and for the first time in too many weeks to count, Zoe let herself relax. "A deal's a deal."

He winked at her. "And since you admire me, you'll come watch me play baseball tomorrow?"

"Yes, Ryan," Zoe replied dutifully, recalling just how he got that tiny scar on his chin. And with a smile to herself, she realized not only did she admire the man Ryan had become, she was beginning to trust him again, too.

Zoe wasn't anxious to broadcast her embarrassing experience at the department store. Yet she wasn't surprised that everyone she spoke to the next afternoon at the high school baseball field knew the full story.

"The Riverbend gossip mill is churning at full force," she groused to Kate. She grabbed one end of the cooler and followed her sister up the bleachers to the top row. It was a bit windier but—she spotted Ryan doing stretches on the field—the view was spectacular.

Kate raised her sunglasses. "Helped considerably by the news report on Channel 2."

"The only person I haven't heard from is Mom." Zoe mentally counted the days. "It's been more than a week. She's never home. She doesn't return phone calls."

Kate motioned Zoe to sit. "I'm sure mother would tell you that she's been out, having a life."

Zoe sat, then reached into the cooler for a diet soda. "I'd be a lot happier if she shared some of that life she's having with us. And *you* shouldn't believe everything you watch on TV."

"I wouldn't have to rely on outside sources if my sister would spill the beans."

"Loose lips sink ships." She took a sip of soda.

Kate groaned. "Next you're going to tell me all's well that ends well."

Zoe brightened. She popped a top on another can of soda, which she handed to Kate. "I wouldn't have thought of quoting Shakespeare, but if it works…"

Kate rolled her eyes and then pushed her sunglasses back in place. "So did my matchmaking efforts."

"You're not matchmaking." Zoe shaded her eyes so she could study him closely. He had walked over to the area designated as his team's dugout, where he stood alone in profile, his arms crossed in front of his chest, a baseball cap slung low on his forehead, shadowing most of his face.

Despite his apparent nonchalance, she didn't need to see his eyes to know they were keenly observing the surroundings. No detail, she thought, large or small, got by Ryan O'Connor.

"He can't take his eyes off you," Kate whispered.

Zoe couldn't take her eyes off him as he walked to the pitcher's mound. When he turned slightly, she saw the number seventeen on the back of his white T-shirt, which hugged his broad shoulders. The royal-blue stitching above the number spelled out his last name. All in all, he made up a sexy package, one any savvy woman would want to claim as hers.

Better not go there, Zoe thought. She turned to Kate. "You're wasting your talents on us. But I think we're on our way to being friends again."

"Uh-huh." Kate didn't bother to hide a smile. "Oh, there's Alec." Kate shouted her fiancé's name. Alec had walked over to Ryan, who'd been kicking at the dirt on the pitcher's mound. Both men looked up in their direction. Alec merely waved, but Ryan jogged across the field and up the bleacher steps until he stood eye-to-eye with Zoe.

He pushed his cap back so she could see his face. His blue eyes twinkled with humor as he nudged a place for himself between her and Kate. "Glad you're here," he said to Zoe. He turned to Kate. "You, too, of course."

"Of course," Kate said dryly. "Shall I clear the stands so the two of you can be alone?" She grabbed her soda, and another can from the cooler, and headed down the bleachers.

"I am glad you're here," Ryan repeated softly. He tucked a few stray strands of her hair behind her ear. His fingers traced the line of her cheek.

Ryan's touch left Zoe inexplicably tongue-tied. Friends, she told herself. "I hadn't expected so many people would come to a community baseball game." She pulled back just enough to break contact. She forced her eyes to wander so she wouldn't have to look at him.

"Just a little rivalry between the high school and the police department," he said. "Alec's pitching for the teachers."

She turned back to him and smiled. She traced the scar on his chin. "A souvenir from the last time I saw you pitch."

"Yeah," he said deadpan. "But at least this time you're not at the plate." He lightly kissed her on the forehead. "Just so I don't forget where to continue." He marked the spot with his forefinger and, with a wink, jogged back down to the field.

She rubbed the spot where his lips had touched. He had to know he was keeping her off balance, and he was enjoying every minute. What was he up to? She tried, unsuccessfully, not to let Kate's words, *he can't take his eyes off you,* mean too much.

Ryan found it impossible to completely focus on the game with Zoe sitting in the stands. It was the bottom of the seventh and he was working on a no-hitter. He'd struck out the first batter and the next man had popped out to center.

He narrowed his gaze and tried to concentrate. But out of the corner of one eye he saw Zoe stand and wave wildly.

The rest of the bleacher crowd joined in, shouting, clapping and stomping so hard he could feel the tremors all the way to the pitcher's mound. He proceeded to walk the next two batters and a wild pitch hit the next man, sending him to first.

Jake, his team's catcher, trotted out to the mound. Jake lifted his faceplate. "Two outs. Bases loaded."

He scowled at Jake and then up into the stands. "Give me a minute." The he heard Zoe shout his name. The crowd took up the chant. *"Ryan. Ryan. Ryan."*

He motioned Jake back to the plate. Alec was the next batter up, and Ryan figured he'd be an easy out. Ryan threw a pitch, aiming for inside and low. Instead, the ball shot out of his hand and directly into the path of Alec's bat. The resounding crack had him wincing as he watched the ball sail out of the field and Alec sprint round the bases. Four-zip.

Silence reigned on his side of the bleachers. The fans in the other bleachers cheered wildly.

From that moment on, Ryan's game continued downhill. His gaze kept straying to the bleachers. It was getting harder to take his eyes off her face, off her legs. Off of Zoe.

He'd been a fool to believe he could keep sex out

of their relationship. He wanted her. He knew she wanted him. The question was, what was he going to do about it?

There were two games being played that afternoon, Zoe thought. On the field, baseball. Off the field, seduction of a sort. As far as Zoe was concerned, there were no rules to the latter.

As to the former, she loved baseball. It was hard not to get caught up in this game, especially with Ryan working on a no-hitter. She couldn't help but notice that Ryan definitely was in terrific shape, all six-feet-plus of him.

Maybe Kate was right in her assessment, that Ryan couldn't keep his eyes off her. Zoe decided to test that theory. She stood, started clapping wildly. The crowd joined in.

Ryan walked the next batter.

She shouted his name. And the crowd picked up the chant.

His pitch clipped the batter on the right shoulder.

Zoe couldn't see Ryan's face clearly, but could tell he wasn't happy with the turn of events. After Alec's home run, which made the score four to zero, Ryan slowly walked off the field, meeting his friend at home plate where the two men exchanged a high-five and walked off the field together.

Zoe remained standing while the rest of her bleacher mates sat. Ryan sauntered over to the bleachers, raised his cap so she could see his face. She started down to meet him, but he silently mouthed the word *later*. Then he smiled.

When Ryan's side struck out one-two-three in the

top of the ninth, making the final score eight-two, Zoe rushed down the bleachers, pushed through the crowd and stepped into his waiting arms.

"That was a wise decision on your part, choosing police work over professional sports." Zoe spread the blanket under the maple tree she'd discovered not far from the baseball field, then sat with her back against the trunk. She grinned at the dumbfounded expression on Ryan's face.

He wiggled his eyebrows and stroked an imaginary mustache. "You're a mighty powerful distraction."

"Even in defeat you were the hero. Kate said the teachers hadn't won a game all season." Zoe unpacked the cooler and handed Ryan, who'd settled next to her, a turkey sandwich just the way she remembered he liked it. A rye roll, thick slices of roast turkey, lots of mayonnaise, two pieces of Swiss cheese, a touch of lettuce and a thin slice of tomato.

"Just part of being a good best man." Ryan grinned, took a bite of the sandwich and nodded his appreciation. "Alec's finding small-town life an adjustment. He was the principal at the biggest high school in Philly until he burned out. Riverbend's a quarter of the size, but he's discovering the problems are much the same."

Zoe unwrapped a roast beef sandwich. "He seems happy here."

"He loves Kate," Ryan said simply. "I think they fell in love the moment they met. They're perfect for each other." He glanced around. "I thought they were right behind us."

"Kate took a slight detour. Said she thought she saw someone she knew. Guess she wanted to introduce him to Alec." Zoe bit into her sandwich—rye roll, medium-rare roast beef, thinly sliced, lots of mayonnaise, two pieces of Swiss cheese, a touch of lettuce and a thin slice of tomato.

She would've been just as satisfied with the turkey. And Ryan wouldn't have complained if she'd offered him the roast beef.

Zoe thought back to Kate's words from more than a week ago. *Time is irrelevant when you're in love. Alec is perfect for me. Like Ryan's perfect for you.*

Zoe didn't believe for a minute that liking the same kind of sandwiches as Ryan meant they were perfect for one another. She'd learned from experience that relationships ebbed and flowed, and it took considerable effort on both parties to make one work. From her viewpoint, unconditional love was something greeting card companies concocted to make more sales.

The truth, as she saw it, was that people constantly walked into and walked out of each other's lives. Wasn't her life proof of that? No relationship was perfect. Which was what she was going to tell Ryan when she realized they were no longer alone.

Ryan had stood, and was quietly talking with Riverbend's mayor, a gregarious-looking man in his late fifties who'd been leading the town for more than twenty years. As the two men shook hands, the mayor said, "If you want the job, son, you just have to say so."

"We agreed on temporary," Ryan reminded him. "Nine months, maybe a year at the most."

"You've done a good job these past six months," the mayor said. "Chief Whitney himself couldn't have done better. Shame about his heart giving out like that. But like him, you know the town, you know the people."

"I'm going back to Philadelphia in a few months."

"But," the mayor persisted, "the council wants you. The town needs you."

The mayor smiled down at Zoe. "Didn't mean to interrupt. Nice to see you again, Zoe. My wife watches you every morning. You let me know what you're thinking, Ryan."

The men shook hands again, and only when the mayor was out of sight did Ryan sit down.

"Will you take the job or go home to Philly?" she asked when it became apparent Ryan wasn't going to talk about the mayor's offer.

"Philly," Ryan replied quickly. "My life's waiting for me back there." Ryan stared at his half-eaten sandwich, wrapped it up and placed it in the cooler. He pulled out a soda, popped the top and took a long drink.

"What's wrong?"

"Just wondering whether I can face the demons waiting for me." He finished his soda and aimed the empty can in the direction of the trash barrel. It hit the rim and dropped inside with a clang.

Zoe waited for him to continue. When he didn't, she pressed on, needing to know the answer to another question. "Anyone besides those demons waiting for you?"

"I'm the only one sharing information," he reminded her with a mildly reproachful look. "No. There's no one special. You?"

"I'm a statistic," she finally said, "one of those you read about in the weekly news magazines. I'm single. Just shy of thirty. Never had a serious relationship. Am goal- and career-oriented."

"Someone swept you off your feet and then dropped you."

Zoe smiled sadly, thinking of Jeremy with the pouty lips.

"You miss him?"

"Good heavens, no!" Zoe shuddered. "He was a walking, talking cliché. Brooks Brothers suits, shirts, ties and shoes. He dripped Wall Street even though he worked on the upper West Side. Jeremy was into status. And I was into noncommitment.

"That suited me just fine, until Kate called with the news she was getting married again. I looked at Jeremy. I looked at my high-profile job that left me so little time to appreciate my tidy little life that I'd worked so hard to organize. And you know what I discovered?"

Ryan turned her to face him. "What did you discover, Zoe?"

She wanted to tell him she'd discovered love at first sight was a fairy tale, but one that she wanted to believe in. That she'd never thought broken relationships could be repaired, until Ryan stepped back into her life.

A week ago she'd been aghast at spending mere minutes with Ryan—especially with jail cell bars between them. Today, as she had yesterday and even the day before, she was enjoying herself, relaxing in his company, admiring him, liking him. They were friends again. Okay, so he could make her sizzle with a look or a smile. She was smart enough to admit that she'd never been kissed quite the way he'd kissed her.

Just friends, she told herself. She couldn't allow herself to risk feeling more. He'd made his feelings perfectly clear. He had his future mapped out. A future that didn't include her. And while she might tell herself she'd take whatever part of him he'd be willing to share, Zoe knew that if she didn't have a solid place in Ryan's heart, she'd never find true happiness with him.

"That my life was filled with acquaintances, not close friends," she said. "Objects, not personal possessions. I've spent the past six years making my own way in the world, taking control so I wouldn't feel abandoned again."

He scrubbed his hands down his face. "Working vice doesn't leave you much time for a personal life. I didn't love 'em and leave 'em. Just made sure I never got in deep enough."

"I can't imagine you alone."

Ryan shrugged. "I chose police work, and it's a career that makes it hard to let people get close. You, Kate and Jake were my best friends growing up."

He thought of Sean. And the pain he'd been carrying around in his heart for the past months. He thought of his parents and how, after they'd died, he'd carried around the pain of loving them, as well. "You weren't the only one who felt abandoned. One day my parents were there, the next day they were gone."

"Maybe we should make a pact," Zoe said impulsively. "Five years from now, if neither of us is married or involved with other people..."

"You're joking, right?" The look on his face pleaded with her to agree.

"Yeah." She sipped on her soda. "Just joking."

"Good." He sounded relieved. "I wouldn't want anything like love or marriage to ever interfere with our friendship."

She wanted to ask why they couldn't have love, marriage *and* a friendship. Zoe cared for Ryan, cared about what happened to him. And long after Kate walked down the aisle with Alec, long after Zoe returned to New York and Ryan...well, wherever Ryan landed, she wanted to know he cared for her, too.

She envisioned the two empty chairs at her graduation ceremony, and discovered the hurt had begun to dull. Why couldn't Ryan put his pain behind him?

"The last few months before graduation were horrible. Mom and Dad were fighting all the time. You and Kate were away at college. I had no one to talk to."

She hesitated, unsure of how to continue. Then the words spilled out. "Dad left me. You and Kate left me. I didn't feel capable dealing with Mother on my own."

Ryan looked at her thoughtfully. "I guess we never considered what you were going through. And I'm sorry. But you survived. And you thrived. You seem happy, content.''

"Most days. I have a small group of friends, more like acquaintances, really,'' she told him. "People to shop with, to go to dinner with, see movies with. But I've learned it's smarter to keep my emotional distance.''

Ryan angled his arm around her shoulders and drew her to him. "You and your dad getting along now?''

Zoe fussed with the sandwiches and sodas in the cooler. "Yes and no. We exchange e-mail. I see him maybe once a year, usually when I'm on assignment. It's been a while since I visited California. My fault,'' she said quickly. "He'd come to New York more if I asked. We speak on the phone but we rarely *talk.*''

She'd never found it easy to discuss her father. But she found she wanted to share her feelings with Ryan. "Mother alternated between totally devastated and totally stoic. She kept telling us how much she loved us, how much he loved us. But if you looked at her closely, her eyes were always filled with tears. She seems happy now. I hope seeing Dad at the wedding doesn't upset her.''

"I was so angry at my parents for dying in that car accident,'' Ryan murmured. "I never had a chance to say goodbye. To tell them how much I loved them. How proud I was to be their son…. At least you know that if you need your father, he's there.''

Zoe stood up, kept her back straight and unbending. "That doesn't change what happened back then.''

"That's true. But at least you have a choice.'' Ryan

understood how this conversation had upset her. He only hoped she'd find some measure of relief, as he was beginning to, in letting go of the past. Yet he wasn't sure of the right words to comfort her, or if she'd accept them if he did. She slowly walked toward him, her eyes rimmed with tears he knew she wouldn't shed, especially in front of him.

After she'd folded the blanket, he stuck it under his arm and together they silently lugged the cooler back to Kate's unlocked car, and stowed it in the trunk.

Zoe silently fussed with the items in the back seat before she abruptly shoved at them. "Mother's going to start dating."

"Good for her."

"Kate and I think *maybe* it will be good for her once you and Alec check the guy out."

He laughed. "Isn't that a bit presumptuous of you two? I can just imagine what Alec had to say."

"I'm sure he wants what's the best for my mother."

"We all do." Ryan started to say more, but was interrupted by his vibrating beeper. He checked the number, and sighed. "It's the station. Can you get home okay?"

"I don't understand," Zoe said plaintively, "where your constant need to play the white knight comes from."

Ryan nudged her across the street. "Scat, before I enlist Jake to drive you home. I'll call you later."

Thoughts about her father kept running through Zoe's mind as she walked briskly back to the house.

She waved to Penelope, who was sitting on the porch swing. She wasn't alone.

Zoe stood on the sidewalk dumfounded. What was Lawrence Russell doing relaxing on the front porch of her family home looking as though he'd never left?

Chapter Seven

Zoe's world tilted off balance and she had no clue how to right it. She stood silently at the foot of the walkway, and stared numbly at her parents, her *divorced* parents. They hadn't seen her yet as they held hands, relaxing on the porch swing, looking like a man and woman in the first bloom of love.

She thought about all the scenarios she'd created in anticipation of Ryan O'Connor bounding back into her life. Zoe never had imagined any scenarios of her mother and father together again. And now that her father was here, she realized just how woefully unprepared she was.

At times like this, she really needed the emotional support of a friend, and Ryan was the only person Zoe could think of—the only person she wanted—with her now. But Ryan wasn't here, and Zoe would have to face her parents all by herself.

Her father looked up as she climbed the steps to the porch. Zoe saw a wariness in his green eyes that she was sure mirrored her own. He reached out, but stopped just short of touching her. "You're looking well, Zoe."

"What are you doing *here* now?" She tried to keep the tone of her voice neutral, and winced when she heard it edge toward hostility, which wasn't her intent. She didn't want to hurt either of them, but she was going to protect her mother at all costs.

"Zoe," Penelope admonished her. "That's no way to speak to your father."

Lawrence wrapped an arm around comfortably around Penelope's shoulder. "Zoe deserves an honest answer."

"And she'll get one," Penelope said. She turned to Zoe. "And I expect you'll keep an open mind." She didn't give Zoe time to answer before continuing. "Your father and I are dating again."

"Dating?" Zoe asked in disbelief. She sank onto the porch steps. "You're *dating?* Dad's your mystery man."

"I called Kate to congratulate her on her engagement," Lawrence said. "Your mother answered the phone. It was good to hear her voice."

"We hadn't talked in so many years," Penelope said.

"We'd forgotten how to have a simple conversation," Lawrence added. He smiled warmly at Penelope. "After we hung up, I called back. Told her I'd like to see her before the wedding. Just to catch up. So I flew out the end of last month."

"We didn't plan to keep it a secret. We know how much the divorce hurt both you and Kate. But we realized that despite our differences, we still have strong…feelings for one another," Penelope said. "And so we're taking the time we need to see if we can be together again." Her mother's hopeful look implored Zoe to accept her decision.

"I won't pretend to understand," Zoe said faintly. "But you're telling me that after ten years apart, you've decided to try and see if you can be together again."

Penelope opened her arms but Zoe shook her head, totally confused. She pulled open the front door and dashed up the stairs to the room that had been hers as a child.

She heard her mother call her name, heard Penelope's footsteps on the stairs, and thought she heard her father calmly say, "Let me talk to her."

Zoe stared out the window at the oak tree. If she climbed into its branches, would she find the solace she'd always had? She longed for the days when she could count on Ryan finding her there, always ready to comfort her.

But nothing in her life was the same as it had been before.

"I know seeing your mother and I together again comes as a shock to you."

"I never understood why you divorced." Zoe squared her shoulders and turned to her father standing in the doorway. She took a good, long look at him. His full head of hair, once the color of a shiny copper penny, was now white. It had been over a year since she'd last seen him. She remembered that he'd seemed old, discontent. But now, like Penelope, he looked younger, happier.

Could her parents find happiness together after all their years apart? Zoe really wanted to know. She was astute enough to understand that when she had the answers to questions about her past she'd be able to deal better with the questions about her future.

She sat on the edge of the window seat, leaving enough room for Lawrence to join her.

For the next several hours, Zoe had a long-overdue talk with her father. He told her that both he and Penelope soon realized they'd married too young, and slowly they grew apart, wanting different things from their marriage. And as the marriage's foundation began to crack, both of them were too stubborn to take the time necessary to patch their relationship, until the marriage crumbled completely.

"We stayed together as long as we could," Lawrence said. "Years longer than we should have. I deeply regret that your mother and I separating, and Kate's elopement with Ryan, came at the same time. You were hurting, and we were all too self-involved to see it."

"For years I thought there was something lacking in me, that all the people I loved left me. I know now," Zoe added hastily as Lawrence began to object, "that wasn't true. But it was how I felt."

"I made lots of mistakes." Lawrence's eyes, deep green and so similar to Zoe's in color and shape, filled with sadness where a twinkle once had lived. "The last ten years have weighed heavily on me. I'm sure it's not easy for you to accept me popping back into your mother's life like this.''

''No, it's not,'' Zoe admitted. ''But that's Mother's decision.''

Lawrence nodded. ''I'd like a chance to make things right with you, Zoe. To be a part of your life again, not just watch from the sidelines.''

The eighteen-year-old Zoe Russell would have tossed her father's words back in his face. Just days ago, the twenty-eight-year-old Zoe might have done the same. But she'd learned something over the past week from Ryan about giving and taking second chances. ''I'd like that, too.''

''I understand Ryan's come back in your life,'' Lawrence continued easily, as though he'd read her thoughts. ''From what your mother tells me, you two are making your peace with one another. About time, if you ask me.''

Zoe bit her lip to keep from smiling, or remembering. She couldn't count how many times, back when she was much younger, when Lawrence sat her on his knee and ended his fatherly lecture with the phrase, *about time, if you ask me.*

''You were always brimming with forgiveness,'' he continued. ''It's not in you to turn your back when someone offers friendship.''

He was, she knew, talking as much about himself as about Ryan. ''I'm rediscovering some of Ryan's more unique qualities,'' Zoe said dryly.

She heard her heart beating in her chest, her little voice ordering her to take that second chance on her father. She saw the hopeful look on his face and discovered that, despite the past hurts, she wanted to forgive him. "You've given me a lot to think about."

Lawrence rose. "Then I'll leave you to your thoughts. We'll talk again tomorrow?" He smiled when Zoe nodded her acceptance.

She waited until she was certain he was down the stairs before she slowly followed. Through the reflection in the hallway mirror, she could see her parents talking quietly at the front door. Her mother rested her head on Lawrence's shoulder, a scene so familiar that Zoe felt her eyes well with tears.

Before she could say a word, her father slipped out the door. Her mother remained at the doorway.

Zoe hugged Penelope fiercely. "I love you very much."

Penelope hugged her back. "And I you. Your father loves you, too. The Russell women have been blessed with second chances." She nudged Zoe out the door. "Now go find yours."

"Is there a problem here?" Ryan braced his arms on the doorway of the small convenience store. He knew the answer before he'd asked the question. His dispatcher's message had been clear and concise. Her teenage son, Howie, clerking at the store right around the corner from the police station, had noticed a man acting strangely and had called in to report it.

The middle-aged man standing in front of the counter turned and froze. Ryan recognized him as Alan Delaney, a normally quiet man with no history of violence who until recently had owned the hardware store on the Town Square. A slow economy, and the rise of superstores, had helped fold his business.

He was cleanly dressed in clothes that were faded and a bit tattered. His face was filled with a haunted look that Ryan guided by his trained policeman's eye, recognized as a combination of fear and resentment.

"I don't want any trouble," said Alan. "Just what's in the cash register."

"How much money is there?" Ryan asked conversationally, keeping one eye on the would-be robber and one eye on Howie, whose entire body shook badly. Ryan was unarmed, and he could only hope that whatever weapon Alan carried, he'd be too afraid to use it. Ryan knew he could defuse this situation without anyone getting hurt. Just as he'd done dozens of times before…before what happened to Sean.

He shook his head to clear it of anything besides the scene playing out before him. This was Riverbend, not Philadelphia. Standing in front of him was a man beaten by a downward economy, not a crafty drug dealer needing to score.

"About…fif-fif-fifty dollars," Howie stuttered.

"I've been out of work months now since the store closed." Alan squared his shoulders and said with total defiance, "I won't apply for welfare and I won't beg on the streets."

"I sympathize with your situation," Ryan said moving toward him slowly, his hands raised to show he had no weapon, and blocking the only means of escape.

Just then, Zoe stepped through the doorway. Ryan maintained his cool, calm, professional demeanor, but irritation flashed in his eyes when he spotted her. His warning glance spoke volumes. He'd deal with the situation before him now. And with her, later.

"And I think we can take care of the problem," Ryan said calmly. "Howie, call Jake at the station. Let him and your mother know that you're not hurt and that everything's under control here."

As Howie placed the call, Ryan reached into his back pocket, took out his wallet and withdrew several bills. He put them in Alan's coat pocket and retrieved the "weapon."

"You have to come down to the station." Ryan held up a bruised and somewhat battered banana.

"I wasn't going to hurt anyone." Alan Delaney said sheepishly, his face turning a shade of bright pink when he saw Zoe. "Don't I know you from TV?"

"That's Zoe Russell from *Wake Up, America*," said Howie, who seemed to recover quickly from the experience. "She used to baby-sit me."

"You're Howie Zimmer?" Zoe was having a hard time reconciling the tall, lanky teenager with the fat and happy baby she used to bounce on her knee. Or that she'd walked into a robbery in progress. One that Ryan had defused without anyone getting hurt.

Ryan laid a hand comfortably on Alan's shoulder. "Why don't you and I take a walk across the street? Zoe and Howie will join us in a few minutes. I'm sure she'll be happy to answer any questions you have about her exciting life on TV."

Zoe slid to Ryan's side and whispered in his ear, "The mayor was right."

"About what?" Ryan said as he cuffed Alan Delaney, then read him his rights.

"You have made a difference here."

Zoe arrived at the station about twenty minutes later with Howie in tow, and once she'd reunited him with his mother, she wandered around Ryan's office while he conferred on the telephone. She tried not to eavesdrop, but she gathered that he was discussing Alan Delaney's situation.

She checked out the plaques on the wall, her appearance in the full-length mirror hanging on the back of his office door, and carefully read the notices on the bulletin board that included the FBI's Ten Most Wanted. She was relieved she recognized none of them.

Feeling restless, she slid into the chair across from Ryan, who was winding up his conversation, and picked up the lone picture on his desk—the one of him with a dark-haired man she instinctively knew was his late partner, Sean.

She examined the photo carefully, noting how they stood shoulder-to-shoulder, like the brothers of the heart she knew they'd been, their faces ever so slightly turned toward each other. In their eyes, on their faces, the camera had captured the strong bonds of friendship.

She shifted her gaze to Ryan's face. His gaze, razor-sharp as always, locked with hers.

"Wanna tell me why you were at the convenience store?" Ryan dropped the phone into its cradle and leaned back in his chair.

"You're a very nice man." Zoe set the photo back in its place. "And today I realized just how much I admire you."

"*You're* evading my question," Ryan shot back.

She could tell it was costing him some effort to keep calm. And she was touched by his concern, although she considered it misplaced. "I was never in any real danger."

Ryan groaned and rubbed his hands down his face. "Alan Delaney may not have had a gun. But he was desperate enough to attempt robbery. You could have been hurt."

She'd been frightened for him, even knowing he had control of the situation. And today, she'd seen a side of Ryan that she'd forgotten.

"I knew you'd protect me," Zoe said earnestly. "Besides, you handled it perfectly. The store wasn't robbed, Mr. Delaney got money he needed, and he kept his dignity. You, however, are out fifty dollars. But I know that's not as important to you as keeping Howie and me, and Mr. Delaney, safe."

Ryan rolled his eyes. When he saw her casually stroll into the store he'd wanted to throttle her. But she'd followed his silent instructions and kept her distance, kept her cool. "Is this Zoe Russell's famous fuzzy logic at work again?"

She came around his desk and perched on the edge of it. Then she leaned over and hugged him.

"What's that for?" Ryan shrugged out of Zoe's embrace. When she was that close, or he was touching her, Ryan's mind couldn't focus.

She tapped the telephone receiver. "You were looking out for Alan Delaney again."

Ryan nodded. "I talked to the district judge, who agreed to waive bail, pending a hearing. Alan's family promised to see that he gets professional help."

"Speaking of families and help," he continued, wishing he knew what was going on in that mind of hers, "you're here to hound me about checking out that man your mother's interested in."

"No need," she said breezily. And smiled.

He looked at her suspiciously. "Care to share? Because a couple of hours ago it topped your to-do list for me."

"The mystery man, who I found sitting on the front porch holding hands with my mother, is my…my father."

Ryan whistled. "Oh, boy. How do you feel about that?"

"Surprised. Confused. Happy." She leaned over and touched her brow to Ryan's. "Definitely confused."

She told Ryan about finding her parents together at Kate's house, of their decision to start dating again, and her heart-to-heart talk with her father. "They're happy," Zoe said with a sigh.

"I hear a but," Ryan said.

Zoe shrugged. "But this wedding keeps shaking loose surprises. I never expected to come home to Riverbend and have you pop back into my life. And then there's my father, handing out advice as though I was still his little girl." She paused and narrowed her gaze. "What are you smiling about?"

"Let's see." He began counting off on his fingers. "We have popped back into each other's lives and we're dealing with the consequences. You will always be his little girl. And you called Riverbend *home*. I see some shifts in your thinking."

Who would have thought, Zoe mused, that her feelings about her family, about Ryan and even her feelings about her hometown would have changed so drastically in less than two weeks.

Even before she left Manhattan, Zoe had been troubled at the frantic pace of her life. All work. No play. Sure, her career was on the upswing, but her personal life was practically nonexistent. As she'd gained success at *Wake Up, America*, she'd started to lose something very important. Zoe Russell.

During the past week and a half in Riverbend, she'd found more than a connection with friends and family. She was finding herself again. And she owed a lot of that to Ryan.

Could I be falling in love with him? Love, not lust. A deep and forever kind of love. She slapped her hand to her mouth so the question wouldn't accidentally tumble out. They were friends. Definitely friends. But not lovers. Even if they'd shared kisses hot enough to melt almost anything.

Zoe strode over to Ryan and hugged him again. And was jolted by that familiar sizzle she'd been feeling every time she'd seen him since she'd faced him wearing handcuffs and mud. They were friends again. On the way to being very good friends. Falling in love would only complicate the situation between them.

But if, and it was a mighty big *if,* she was falling

in love with Ryan, Zoe was going to take her time and figure out exactly what she wanted to do about him.

Ryan was hot and bothered. Hot, because having Zoe in his arms had him thinking about being alone with her, kissing her and making love with her. Bothered, because this was neither the time nor the place. His feelings remained the same—he liked her, he cared for her—and so had his decision *not* to act on those feelings.

He couldn't help remembering that he *used* to think of her as his little sister. But Zoe Russell was all grown up. The smart course, the prudent course, the safe course, would be to ease her out of his embrace and send her on her way home. But when she sighed in contentment and leaned her head on his shoulder in a gesture of familiarity and trust, Ryan knew he was a goner. He just wasn't sure what to do about it. About her.

Then Zoe nibbled on his ear.

Ryan shot to his feet, barely catching Zoe before she hit the floor. "What was *that* for?"

"Just hoping to get your attention."

"You got it." He stepped back just enough to keep what he hoped was a safe distance between them. The impish smile on her face had him worried about what she might do next. He frantically searched his mind for something equally harmless to talk about. He couldn't think of a thing. Every image that came to mind had her lying on his bed with her beautiful red hair tousled, her green eyes dark and dreamy, her lips swollen from his kisses. Way past R-rated and well into the X zone.

"Well. Th-then." He mentally pulled himself together. He was an experienced thirty-two-year-old man surely able to deal with—what had Jake called her?—the all-too-tempting red-haired Valkyrie standing in front of him.

She was testing him, and Ryan was very much afraid he was failing the test. "Don't you have some bridesmaid thing to do with Kate at home?" Ryan grabbed her hand and pulled her out of his office, through the station lobby and to the front door.

"You're trying to get rid of me," she accused and managed to brace herself in the doorframe.

"Yes. No." He scrubbed his hands down his face. The "tut-tut" he heard from the dispatcher sitting at her desk reminded him they weren't alone. "Don't *you* have some work to do?" he asked the woman coolly.

"You two are much more entertaining than anything on TV," the dispatcher said with a small smile. She pointed to the monitor hanging from the ceiling showing a blond, tanned couple wearing little more than bathing suits in a clench so tight that steam rose from their bodies. "And, Ryan," she added giving a nod toward the cell area, "don't forget to take care of your guest."

He tugged on Zoe's arm, giving her no choice but to follow him. She was grateful for the diversion. "We'll be back in the cell area if anyone needs me."

"You're *not* going to arrest me again." Zoe shivered at the memory that last time she'd been an invited guest in Riverbend's jailhouse nearly two weeks ago. Mud and handcuffs came to mind. And how she'd carefully guarded her heart from anything having to do with Ryan.

Today she was almost ready to hand that same heart, one that had mended but still felt fragile, over to him on a silver platter, knowing he'd probably toss her heart away rather than keep it. This all grown up Ryan, handsome and virile, affected her as no other man she'd ever met.

But she was going back to Manhattan in a few days. He'd be heading back to Philadelphia to resume his dangerous life there.

"No arrest," he said with a smile. "Trust me."

They were *friends,* and trust was an important part of friendship, Zoe thought as she followed him into the cell area. And the last thing Zoe wanted was to mess up this friendship again. Teasing him, tempting him, making him admit that he wanted her had been one thing. Falling in love with him was another.

If she could so easily fall in love with Ryan, she could just as easily fall out of love with him. Good. Now that that was settled she tossed a brief look his way and only found him gazing at her, thoughtfully. It was at times like these Zoe wished she could read male minds.

But it was a heck of a lot better that she couldn't.

He opened the cell door and ushered her inside. She heard a high-pitched bark come from a small box in the corner and her face broke into a wide grin.

"A puppy!" She stepped closer and watched as the

golden retriever stood on its hind legs, its oversize paws pressed against the side of the box. She itched to pick it up. "Oh, he's adorable."

She leaned over and stroked the puppy's soft fur and was rewarded with a wet kiss on the hand. "Another Webster?" she asked, referring to the puppy he'd had as a young boy.

"A very distant relative." Ryan sat cross-legged on the floor and motioned for Zoe to join him. "This one's about eleven weeks old."

"Can I hold him? He is a him?" Zoe picked up the puppy and cradled him in her arms. The puppy made himself comfortable and closed its eyes. "He's precious."

"A few steps away from being precious," Ryan said dryly. He tickled the puppy under its chin. The puppy's eyes shot open and he leaped from Zoe's arms and slid across the floor. "And not quite trained."

The puppy, which was busy exploring the cell, turned in their direction and barked what Ryan took for his agreement. The puppy bounded over and plopped back onto Zoe's lap.

Ryan reached under the cot, found the leash and snapped it onto the puppy's collar. He stood and helped Zoe up. The puppy, happy with all the attention, ran around the two of them, wrapping the leash around their legs. Once Ryan disentangled the leash, the puppy raced out the cell door, then turned back toward them and barked.

"Wanna let him walk you?" Ryan asked.

Zoe took the leash and found herself yanked forward. "For a little puppy, he's got loads of power."

"He's a lot like Webster was at that age. All paws."

"We keep calling him 'he,'" Zoe said. "What's his name?"

"I was hoping you'd name him."

"Naming him is a big step," Zoe declared as they made their way toward Kate's house. "The wrong name could mar this poor puppy for life."

"Well, then," Ryan said gravely, "you'd better come up with a name fast."

"Why me?"

"Because you owe me a big favor for saving your life at the convenience store." He stooped down in front of the puppy. "Women," he said with mock disgust. "How quickly they forget."

Zoe leaned over to cover the puppy's ears. "Don't listen to him, puppy."

"And if you don't help—" Ryan stood and they continued walking "—he'll have you to blame when he goes to the dog therapist and yowls about how his behavioral problems are all because you didn't name him."

They'd stopped in front of Ryan's old house. Although Zoe clearly understood the emotional reasons Ryan had bought the house and wanted to live in it for a short time, she was confused about what he planned to do with it once he returned to Philadelphia.

She gazed around the yard. The For Sale sign was gone. The roses were still in bloom. The bushes looked smartly trimmed. The house looked ready to become a home to its new residents, Ryan and the puppy.

And then she saw the small van parked in the driveway. A man about her age, who she recognized from high school, came out the front door and locked it. He looked up, saw them, waved and jogged down the walkway.

"We placed all the furniture like you indicated," the man said as he handed Ryan the key.

"I thought you got rid of everything after..." Zoe's voice trailed off. He didn't need a reminder about what had happened after his parents died.

"I put a few pieces into storage." He took the leash from her and untangled it from around their legs. He opened the door and the puppy bounded inside, skidded around the newly polished hardwood floors, finally settling on a pile of pillows nestled against one corner of the living room.

The freshly painted room was pretty bare. She watched as Ryan walked around the room, one by one touching the loveseat, the wooden chair, the knee-high chest and the floor lamp, marking each item as his.

Zoe wondered when he was going to realize that with the puppy and the house he was putting down roots here in Riverbend.

Chapter Eight

The steaming hot water was just the way Ryan liked it, and when he stepped into the shower he braced his hands against the tiles, lowered his head and let the sharp needles of spray dance across his neck and down his back.

It had been, to borrow a phrase from Zoe, a big-drama day. And he'd dealt with all of it in a calm, professional manner. Well, mostly all of it, he thought wryly.

Many years ago, Ryan had pledged to uphold the law, and while Alan Delaney had intended to rob the convenience store, Ryan knew asking the district judge to consider probation rather than jail time for the man was the right course of action. He awarded himself a few bonus points because Zoe considered him a hero and his ego could stand the boost.

He then subtracted those points for having lusty

thoughts about her from the moment that he'd laid eyes on her in the Riverbend jail. He'd spent too much time trying to convince himself there was nothing wrong with them kissing each other senseless.

They were friends again. He didn't want to do anything to lose the trust she had in him. He'd order pizza. They'd have dinner. They'd name the puppy.

He was looking forward to spending the evening with her.

Almost like when they were younger. Except now they were both older, hopefully a bit wiser. They'd made mistakes. They'd learned from them, hadn't they? And weren't they entitled to a second chance? This time Ryan wasn't going to make any mistakes in his second chance friendship with Zoe.

He'd lost too many people in his life; he'd let too many friendships crumble. Not this time. He was going to grab that second chance with Zoe and make the most of it.

He frowned. There was all that chemistry swirling between them. He was no more ready to tumble into an emotional relationship with her—or any other woman—than she was ready for a physical relationship with him. And the latter, Ryan thought grimly as he turned his face up into the shower, was all he could offer her right now. There'd been women in his life, women who always wanted more than he'd been able to give them at the time. Yet he'd always hoped that some day he'd meet the right woman for him. And they'd live happily ever after.

That was before. Before Sean's death, and the role he'd played in it, had tied him up in knots that he wasn't convinced could ever be unraveled. He cared for Zoe, deeply, but he was smart enough to know love didn't magically happen overnight, that sizzle and chemistry were only part of the equation.

For a moment, Ryan let his imagination run free. Zoe stood outside the bathroom door, and through the semitransparent shower curtain he watched the doorknob slowly turn.

She'd come inside, her steps at first hesitant, then a bit bold.

He'd push aside the curtain. The smile on her face would be for him. Her eyes, lit with love, would be for him.

And he'd take her into his arms, kiss her, touch her, make her his, forever.

Whoa! He shook his head to clear it of an X-rated scene that was becoming all too frequent. Ryan turned off the water, stepped out of the shower and wrapped a towel around his waist. He swiped his hand across the mirror, clearing enough of a spot to stare at his reflection. He didn't know what he expected to find, other than the face of a thirty-two-year-old cop searching for a little peace, a little quiet and a little stability.

They needed to talk, all right. That X-rated scene he'd been imagining brought to mind the last time he'd kissed Zoe, a kiss that promised a lot more than either of them were ready for emotionally or physically.

Ryan moved into the bedroom, and as he dressed quickly in a pair of faded jeans and T-shirt, he knew that the unexpected passion still smoldered between them. And that was a problem. A big problem, with no clear solution in sight.

Zoe and the pizza delivery boy arrived at Ryan's house at the same time. She paid for the large deluxe, added a generous tip and used the key Ryan had given her to open his front door.

The puppy, carrying a rolled-up sock in its mouth, greeted her. He danced around in circles, yelping playfully, then bounded up the stairs. Zoe laid the pizza on the bottom step and followed him.

She slid to a stop when she saw the golden retriever plop down in front of the closed door to the master bedroom, now Ryan's room.

Zoe heard the shower running and smiled at the implied intimacy. What would Ryan do if she boldly stepped inside his bedroom, marched into the bathroom, tore the shower curtain away and had her way with him? Zoe slapped her hand to her mouth to stifle the giggle that threatened to spill out. *Have her way with him?*

She sounded like the heroine right out of a historical romance novel.

Ryan stirred her senses, like no man had done before. He made her want…want *things*—like a husband to love and cherish, children to bear and raise, a family to belong to—things she'd found it difficult to imagine she could ever have in the life she'd built for herself in New York City. Things she'd been afraid to think too much about before Ryan O'Connor bounced back into what she'd thought of as a well-planned, well-ordered life.

When Zoe thought about her future, she considered it in terms of her career, not her personal life. Today, *Wake Up, America*, later this week, her first prime-time entertainment special. And, if she was lucky, the special would do well in the ratings and she could write her own ticket at the network.

That's what she wanted. That *was* what she wanted, she thought wryly as she sat down on the top step and relaxed against the newel post. She watched the puppy chew on the sock, considering the number of unexpected curves in the road she'd taken over the past two weeks.

And the most dangerous curve was Ryan O'Connor.

Oh, he'd be amused that she considered him a curve on the road of her life. Just as Zoe was sure she was an unexpected bump on his. He claimed he wanted friendship. She wanted more, much more.

Despite knowing the pitfalls, she was falling in love with Ryan. And she smiled at the thought of locking lips with the all-too-virile man himself, wearing little more than a towel, or maybe nothing at all, around his waist.

Zoe thought about his body, touching his muscles honed from workouts, his broad chest, narrow hips, long runner's legs…. What would it be like to have a man like Ryan madly, hopelessly in love with her?

She shivered, with the pleasure of the thought and the giddy feeling that suddenly had come over her.

"Care to share what's making you grin like a cat who's swallowed the proverbial canary?"

"Ryan! I—" She scrambled to her feet, smoothed

the nonexistent wrinkles on her slacks. He was, thankfully, wearing more than a towel. His white T-shirt was tucked into faded jeans. His hair was still damp from his shower, and he hadn't bothered to shave. The stubble on his cheek made him look sexy and dangerous. Much too dangerous. She needed to keep her wits about her. Ryan had a sneaky way of disarming her defenses when she least expected it.

"Nothing important," Zoe lied as she lunged for the puppy, now playfully running in circles around the two of them. "I think he has business outside. We'll be right back."

I will not blush, Zoe told herself fiercely. But she felt the inevitable heat rise from her chest, staining her cheeks a bright red. She turned to hide her face, flushed from the heat of arousal, and held tightly on to the puppy, all too conscious of Ryan merely a step behind her on the stairs.

She quickened her pace and in the minute or two it took for her to leave the house and reach the far end of the yard, she was back in control. Her face had cooled. Her heartbeat had returned to its normal rhythm. She could tell herself a thousand times that Ryan used to tease her like this when they were younger, but now each of them was more aware of the other in a truly adult fashion.

The idea thrilled her as much as it scared her. While she had no trouble imagining what it would be like belonging with and to Ryan, the reality was a lot more dangerous to her heart.

"I know you, Zoe, you don't blush over nothing," Ryan laughingly called from the back door.

Ignoring him seemed the smartest course of action for the moment. Zoe followed the puppy around the yard until the golden retriever finished his business and romped over to the back door where Ryan waited.

"I don't know how you do it," she muttered loud enough so Ryan could hear, "but with just a word you make my knees turn to jelly and drive all thoughts except of you out of my mind."

"There's nothing to be embarrassed about." He grinned. "Like I told you before, chemistry."

"I'm not embarrassed, just confused. And to set the record straight, I…" She paused. "Women have fantasies, too. You got with a problem with that?"

"Not at all. It's a boost to my ego that your fantasies are about me." His stomach growled when she punched it. "But I'm a realist. So it's pizza first, fantasies later," he said, and let her ease out of his grasp.

Zoe wisely let go of the conversational thread. "Not much has changed in this house since we were kids."

She followed him into the kitchen, wishing she could read his mind. He seemed like Jekyll and Hyde, one side playfully romantic, the other emotionally distant.

"I take that back," she said. "I don't remember the linoleum floor being so faded and scratched. And why would anyone paint wood cabinets such a bright…would you call that color yellow?"

"I'd call it someone's idea of a bad breakfast joke," Ryan replied.

Zoe vividly recalled the day she'd helped Ryan's mother hang the homemade curtains trimmed in lace over the two windows—one over the chipped porcelain sink and the other in the small dining area—where Zoe, Kate and Ryan used to eat macaroni and cheese. Today those windows were covered with plastic miniblinds.

Zoe let her gaze roam the room. "The whole house could use some TLC before anyone could call it home."

"Right now I've got the time and the money to do just that," Ryan said cheerfully. He took several slices out of the box and placed them into the small microwave that sat alone on the countertop. He opened a cabinet and took out paper plates. When the microwave pinged, he placed the slices on two paper plates. "Plastic forks are in that drawer over there. Beer and soda's in the fridge."

He led her to the living room and set the pizza down on the small chest he was using as a coffee table. As Zoe settled on one side of the loveseat, the puppy jumped up and cuddled at her side, its nose resting on its paws. "The last time we shared pizza I was tempted to toss the entire box at you."

"And then we played a mean game of Truth or Dare." He rubbed his cheek. "I'm still feeling the pain from all those verbal jabs you threw at me."

"Those well-deserved verbal jabs," Zoe said as she sipped on a diet soda. No beer for her tonight. She needed to keep a clear head around Ryan.

Ryan grabbed the wooden chair, turned and straddled it so he faced Zoe. "We need to talk. About that kiss."

"Which one?" she asked cheekily.

"Be serious," he admonished her. He started to
take a pull from his beer, but instead placed it on the
table and crossed his arms over the top of the chair.
"You know what I'm talking about. The day we got
a little carried away."

"You're going to sit there and *dissect* our kiss?"
She didn't bother to keep the shock out of her voice.
She remembered that kiss—no, make that *series* of
kisses that ended with her almost melting into a puddle at his feet.

"So you're never going to kiss me again?"

He nodded. "In that way."

"And which way is that?" She had to ask, but she
didn't really want to know. And was somewhat relieved when he didn't answer her. But when the silence in the room grew uncomfortable, she found herself asking again.

"Which way?" she demanded. "The way a man
kisses a woman when he feels something for her? The
way you kissed me a couple of days ago and we both
burst into flame?"

"Yes," he said simply.

She looked at him closely and saw something in
his eyes she couldn't define, but told her that he'd
made up his mind that they were going to be friends,
only friends, and nothing she said or did wasn't going
to change it. "Ryan, what's going on here?"

"You asked me to be honest. I'm trying to be as
honest with you as I can." The words came out much
too stilted, so unlike Ryan, as though he'd just started rehearsing them and was having trouble memoriz-
ing them.

Zoe pulled a face. "I can't believe we're having this conversation."

"Zoe, we're friends again, patching up a relationship that two weeks ago I would have sworn was impossible to fix." The words came out of his mouth so earnestly that for a moment he reminded her of the twelve-year-old boy who'd carried her into the house after she'd fallen out of the oak tree. The boy who'd been her best friend and who'd grown into the man she'd dreamed of a future with.

But the memory lasted just for a moment. Because then he said, "I care for you, deeply. I don't want to hurt you in any way. But there's not going to be a happily-ever-after for us."

He paused, and the pained look in his eyes sent a shiver up and down her body. Whatever he was going to say, Zoe knew instinctively that she didn't want to hear it.

"I'm not going to fall in love with you."

Bingo! She felt her heart bump, stop and then slowly begin to beat again. She hurt all over. She drew in a deep breath, let it out slowly, and tried to force the pain out along with it. But she couldn't. She'd expected the battle to win Ryan's heart would be an uphill one, but she'd never, ever expected to be told, straight out that he wasn't *ever* going to fall in love with her.

She felt her defenses rise. "I hadn't realized that a *mere* kiss was the first step to falling in love. So explain this to me. You're not going to fall in love with me because you can't, or because you don't want to, or because you're in love with someone else. All or none of the above?''

''Does every conversation with you have to be a battle?'' he asked.

''Of course not,'' she replied crossly. ''They just need to make sense.''

She stood quickly, keeping her hands fisted at her side in fear that she might give in to the mounting desire to slug him where it might do the most damage. ''The last time we had this conversation about kisses, shortly before you saved my butt in Cincinnati, you were concerned that whatever was happening between us—don't worry, I won't call it love—wouldn't affect the roles we're playing in Kate and Alec's wedding.''

''Don't pretend you don't remember what I told you that day.''

''Yes. I remember. Your feelings about losing Sean. Your feelings about your job. Your feelings about yourself. Your feelings about me. And I bared all my feelings to you. That's what friends do. And so, Ryan, I am thrilled that you're getting in touch with your feelings.''

''There's no need to be sarcastic.'' He sounded affronted.

Zoe plopped back onto the loveseat so abruptly that she dislodged the puppy at her side but managed to catch him before he slid onto the floor. ''You're right. Every time we try and sort out our relationship, I feel as though we're doing a George Burns-Gracie Allen routine. And that we're speaking in different languages.''

''What are you talking about?''

"Male." She pointed to him. "Female." She pointed to herself. "And you," she told the puppy, "I'm going to name you Chance."

"What kind of name is Chance for a puppy?"

She shot Ryan a look that would freeze a glacier. She needed some time to think about what she was going to do about him. About them. Because she knew for sure she wasn't going to give up on Ryan O'Connor. "Think about it."

"Keep away from all women until you're old enough to understand them," Ryan said, tugging on Chance's leash as the puppy lunged happily toward the chocolate-brown toy poodle sitting primly behind the clapboard fence. The puppy's name had stuck, because Ryan knew exactly what Zoe had meant. He'd come very close to risking that second chance they'd been given.

"Which means," he continued, "you'll be buried before you do." They were almost done with their late afternoon walk around the block, something Ryan found he enjoyed immensely. He would have enjoyed it even more if Zoe had joined them, but Ryan hadn't seen her for the past few days. He'd see her tonight at the wedding rehearsal. He knew she expected an apology. He just wasn't sure why he needed to apologize for being honest. Especially when she'd demanded honesty.

He slowed his pace as they passed Kate's house just at the moment Zoe came out the door. Ryan had never seen a more stunning woman, simply dressed in dark green linen slacks and a lighter green sweater that brought out the deep green of her eyes and the luxurious red of her hair. The mild breeze blew through her hair, and she tucked an errant curl behind her ear.

"Hi there, Chance." She leaned over and petted the golden retriever, who barked happily. "He's looking mighty happy," she said to Ryan.

"He's missed you." *I've missed you.*

"If you've got places to go and people to see, don't let me stop you," she said breezily. "I don't mind walking him. I've got some time on my hands between now and Monday."

"What's Monday?" The puppy pulled on the leash, but Ryan didn't move. He was afraid if he started walking in one direction, Zoe would take off in the other.

"I fly back to New York. Back to my life." She paused as if to let that news settle. "So, how's Chance doing?"

"In less than a week he's gnawed on more articles of my clothing than I can count," Ryan said, following her lead in playing it cool, although he felt far from relaxed. There was still so much left unsaid between them he didn't know where to begin. He didn't know how to begin. "He may be off to puppy training school."

"You should know better than to leave anything chewable in sight." Zoe smiled, but the smile didn't reach her eyes as she leaned over to scratch Chance behind the ears. "He reminds me so much of Webster with his big paws and floppy ears and a tail that never stops wagging."

"I threatened Webster with training school, too."
Ryan crouched down in front of the puppy. "You're
an all-right dog, Chance, even if you did eat my favorite tennis shoes."

"Well, I've got to be going." Zoe started off in
the opposite direction. "I don't want to be late for
the wedding rehearsal."

"Wait." Ryan grabbed her by the elbow. "I've
been meaning to call you."

She said nothing but the pointed look she gave him
asked him why.

Threads of impatience ran through him. She could
be so stubborn. "I saw your promo spot this morning
on *Wake Up, America.*" Ryan grabbed Chance's
leash before the puppy could wander into the street.
"Very impressive. I bet the ratings will go through
the roof tonight."

"My father's going to stand at the back of the
church, and before he lets anyone in he's going to
make sure they've set their VCRs to tape my special."

Zoe glanced at her watch, then back at Ryan. "I'll
see you at the church."

Ryan watched her disappear around the corner. He
tried to hurry the puppy along, but Chance had other
ideas, finding it necessary to stop at every tree on the
block and sniff every leaf on the sidewalk.

It took another ten minutes before Ryan was able
to settle the puppy down for the night, change his
clothes and race over to the wedding rehearsal.

His short conversation with Zoe had left him
strangely unsettled. He didn't like the feeling at all.

* * *

Zoe walked the scenic route through town to the wedding rehearsal at the small church where Kate would be married the next day. She wasn't looking forward to the upcoming evening. She was happy for Kate and Alec, she was coming to terms with her parents' new relationship, but she still felt unsettled over what to do next about her confusing relationship with Ryan.

She loved every part of him, even that stubborn streak that had him believing there was something lacking inside him that prevented him from loving. She understood his anguish over all the losses in his life—his parents, Sean, Kate and even their friendship.

She also knew that Ryan was a smart man, a methodical man, one who had to come to terms with those losses before he could let himself love again. He said he cared for her, that he didn't want to hurt her, that he valued their friendship.

It was obvious they couldn't solve the problems of the past ten years over two weeks. But tonight, she thought as a smile filled her face, she was going to give him a sample of what they could be together, if only he'd give them a chance.

Zoe entered the church and saw her father staring into the mirror in the vestibule, fidgeting with his tie. Over the past few days she'd watched as the bond between her parents grew more solid. While neither of them spoke aloud about reconciling, Zoe wasn't going to be surprised if she was invited to another wedding a few months from now.

In the meantime, Lawrence continued to try and reach out to her, and Zoe was trying hard to accept his overtures, as well as extend a few of her own.

She came up in front of him and straightened his tie, just like she'd done a thousand times…before. "You look very handsome," she said.

Her father winked. "Just takes the love of a good woman. You don't look so bad yourself, Zoe," he teased. "How does it feel to be walking down the aisle in a few minutes."

"As the maid of honor, not the bride," Zoe pointed out. "Although Kate suggested Ryan and I walk down the aisle in place of her and Alec for the rehearsal. I couldn't talk her out of it."

"I had a little chat with Ryan a few days ago."

"Did you now?" Zoe yanked on his tie. "Rule number one. No parental interference."

"How about some advice?" Lawrence asked.

Zoe smiled. "I'll consider any you have to offer as long as you don't mention Ryan by name. We're in battle mode at the moment."

"That's my girl." Lawrence nodded approvingly. "I know you, Zoe, better than you know yourself. You're determined and driven. You get that from me. Thankfully, you get your common sense from your mother."

She yanked on his tie again. "I'm still waiting for your advice."

"Listen to your heart," he said simply. "It won't ever let you down."

From the side of the chapel, Zoe observed all the players assembling for the wedding rehearsal. The bride and groom, Kate and Alec, huddled in the corner, Kate's body language showing some distress, Alec's face covered by a frown.

Just nerves, Zoe decided, as she turned her gaze on her parents, now sitting in the front pew, holding hands and giggling like teenagers. She brushed a tear from her eye.

Sitting a few pews back were Kate's two bridesmaids, oblivious to anything or anyone other than Alec's younger brothers, who were his ushers.

Zoe scanned the room and saw Alec's parents talking with the minister. "Call us Rachel and Tom, we're family now," they'd ordered as they'd hugged the stuffing out of her.

And then she saw Ryan. He stood at the back of the room, his blond hair windblown, lending him a somewhat rakish look. His gaze scanned the room and she knew when he saw her, his eyes lit, his lips curved in a smile. But he kept his distance. Instead, he walked up the center aisle to where Kate sat. He hugged her, then kissed Penelope on the cheek and patted Lawrence on the back before he took his place at the front of the chapel, where he was standing in for the groom during the rehearsal.

Zoe kept her eye on him as she waited for her father, who'd be walking her down the aisle.

Lawrence made it to her side as strains of the wedding march filled the small room, and Zoe hooked her arm through her father's as she walked down the aisle, slowly, step by step, until she reached the man of her dreams.

And listened to her heart.

As the minister explained what the bride and groom would do next, she imagined what it would be like to walk down the aisle for real, dressed in satin and lace, wearing her mother's wedding veil. And when she reached the end of the aisle, her father would place her hand into Ryan's hand.

Zoe smiled. How hard could it be to get Ryan to listen to his heart?

Chapter Nine

The party was in full swing by the time Zoe arrived at the Café on the River. As she stepped through the doorway, she was greeted by the sounds of raucous laughter, the underlying hum of people talking and the sounds of soft jazz from the popular Cincinnati quartet Kate was especially fond of.

"Zoe, where have you been?" Penelope hugged her tightly around the waist and drew her into the intimate banquet room. "I've been looking all over for you."

She held out her right hand and Zoe just stared, unable to find the words to describe the sparkling ring of diamonds encircling her mother's fourth finger.

"It's beautiful. From Dad?" Zoe asked tentatively, her head spinning. "Of course it's from Dad." She narrowed her gaze on her mother. "What does it mean?"

Penelope laughed. "A friendship ring for a special friendship." She laughed again. "I feel as giddy as a schoolgirl. Isn't it grand to have second chances?"

Before Zoe could reply, Lawrence Russell whisked her mother onto the dance floor. The smile Penelope gifted Lawrence with was filled with love, and Zoe couldn't deny that her mother was happy. Or that her father seemed totally besotted with Penelope, more so than Zoe could remember him ever being while they were married. She wished them well, and wished she could find the same measure of contentment for herself.

Zoe continued to search the crowded room for Ryan. She'd lingered at the church hoping to talk privately with him, but by the time she'd been able to break away from an impromptu discussion with Kate's bridesmaids over the merits of pink roses versus yellow, a subject Zoe wasn't able to warm to, Ryan had left.

She wanted to have a heart-to-heart talk with him, to make him understand the depth of her feelings and that she'd take any part of his heart he was able to give her. But during her walk from the church to the restaurant, she was somewhat relieved they hadn't talked because she had decided she wasn't willing to settle for a part of his heart. She wanted all of him. Because she loved him.

It was long past time that she said the words she needed to say and that Ryan needed to hear. And she would, she told herself as she accepted a glass of champagne from a wandering waiter, if he ever showed up.

She'd even got the restaurant hostess, a woman she'd gone to high school with, to promise to let her know the moment he arrived. She'd thought about calling him on his cell phone, but decided she didn't want to seem that anxious to see him. Even if she *was* that anxious to see him.

Kate gave her a hug as Zoe joined her at the head table. "You missed Dad's toast to Mother's charms, my good fortune in finding Alec and your brilliant career. Where've you been?"

"Looking for Ryan." With the tines of her fork, Zoe picked at the plate of filet of sole and shoestring potatoes the waiter placed in front of her. The food looked wonderful but she wasn't hungry. "Where's Alec?"

"I'm sure he's here somewhere," Kate said so absently that Zoe wasn't certain if her sister was talking about Ryan or her husband-to-be. "I hadn't realized we had so many out-of-town guests." Kate sighed. "I hadn't realized how stressed out I am."

"You need a good night's sleep, which you probably won't get until after your honeymoon." Zoe focused on how subdued her sister sounded, not at all like an excited bride-to-be. The frown marring Kate's face worried her. It was the same look she'd seen earlier that day, prior to the wedding rehearsal.

"I haven't slept well in days," Kate confessed. She looked like she wanted to say more, but just shrugged. "Nerves, I guess."

Now—with all the people around and little chance for privacy—wasn't the best time to try and find out what was bothering Kate, but Zoe was determined to get some answers later that night.

"When we get home, I'll make us hot chocolate and we can gossip until dawn if you want. Well, maybe not until dawn," she said. "There's a lot I have to do for you before you walk down the aisle for real tomorrow evening."

Zoe raised her goblet of champagne and touched it to the wineglass in Kate's hand. "So here's my toast to you on your last night as a free woman."

"To me," Kate said weakly, but before she could lift the glass to her lips, she was spirited away for a dance by a man who identified himself as an uncle on Alec's side of the family. Kate hadn't returned by the time that the waiters began clearing the dishes and setting up urns of coffee and pots of hot water for tea. On the table in front of Ryan's still-empty seat lay his untouched salad. Where could he be?

"It won't do to have the maid of honor frowning the night before the wedding." She felt a hand on her shoulder and turned to see her father. "What's the matter?" Lawrence followed her gaze to Ryan's empty chair. "I'm sure he got caught up with something at the police department and he'll be here as soon as he can. Meanwhile, you can show your old man some of those fancy moves you've learned in New York City."

Lawrence offered his hand, and Zoe took it and they walked onto the dance floor.

"That's a beautiful ring you gave Mom."

"Your mother is as lovely as she is forgiving,"

Lawrence said as he expertly moved them across the dance floor until the music stopped.

Zoe leaned her head against her father's shoulder. "I've missed you."

Lawrence kissed her on the forehead. "I've missed you, too. And that's a good beginning for us. Now go find that young man of yours."

Zoe brightened when she saw Kate back at their table. But her sister sat alone, and was looking even more miserable than before. Zoe pushed her way through the crowd of people on the dance floor, but by the time she returned, Kate's seat was empty again.

"The best course of action," Zoe muttered to herself, "would be to sit down and wait for everyone to show up." Zoe sat and idly picked up her half-filled glass of champagne. She sipped slowly, letting the bubbles tickle her nose, feeling the tangy liquid coat her throat, feeling the goose bumps rise on her arms.

The latter reaction wasn't only from the champagne.

Zoe lifted her gaze and saw him. That all-too-sexy and all-too-dangerous man who'd just walked in the door. The man who meant everything to her. More than her career. More than being a celebrity. Because without Ryan, Zoe knew she was only half of whom she was meant to be.

Zoe felt her heart thumping wildly in her chest. And thought about what her father had said, what her heart had been telling her all along.

With a smile on her face, she got up from her seat and headed in Ryan's direction.

Some men looked sexy in a tux, some sexy in jeans

faded in all the right places, some men—and Zoe had to work hard to keep from grinning—in a towel and some men just looked sexy no matter what they were wearing.

Ryan was one of *those* men.

"I think I've danced with every man here but you," she said as she moved in front of him. Her eyes challenged him to say no.

His lips curved in a dangerous smile.

"Dance with me," he ordered softly. He took her hand and pulled her so close that she could hear the beat of his heart. As he slowly maneuvered them around the room, he pressed her head to his chest, resting his palm along the curve of her neck.

Zoe nestled closer, bringing her hips into contact with the part of him guaranteed to let her know just how she was affecting him. Ryan's heart beat faster and his body stiffened.

Good, she had him exactly where she wanted him—hot, bothered and just a touch uncomfortable with those feelings.

"What do you think you're doing?" he choked out. He tried to put some distance between them but Zoe wrapped her arms around his neck.

"Dancing." She looked up at his face, saw his eyes darken, his lips thin. And she gave him a look so innocent she almost felt guilty for what she was about to put him through.

She loved him. She was going to fight for him. And she was sure this was going to be one of their more interesting battles.

"Not in public."

"You don't want to dance in public?"

His voice was like steel. "You know exactly what I mean."

She laughed. "Then come outside with me. To talk." She bumped his hip with hers. "To make up."

"I told you…"

She rolled her eyes. "I remember exactly what you told me. I'm about to have it engraved on a pendant that I'll wear around my neck until I'm old and gray and withered and bouncing someone else's grand-children on my knee. Come outside with me," she cajoled him. "Unless you're afraid…"

"Of you? Never!" But the look on his face told her he wasn't unaffected. He took her hand, and ushered her through the maze of dancing couples to where they could be alone. Ryan closed the French doors and stood with his back to them.

A sliver of moonlight fell across the terrace as he pulled Zoe into his arms.

His lips touched hers gently once, then again before his hand cupped her chin, angling it just right so when he deepened the kiss Zoe felt the warmth spread throughout her body.

Her hands roamed Ryan's back restlessly, finally gliding up to the nape of his neck, capturing the thick, soft strands of his hair.

He kissed her again. Lips to lips. Tongue to tongue. Weak in the knees, she tightened her grasp and closed her eyes as his arms came around her protectively, wrapping her in a cocoon that had to be one of love.

His kiss tasted sweet and salty. All she could think of was that he was exactly what she wanted. What she needed. His touch felt new, but was tenderly familiar.

Wasn't it wonderful, she thought as she let the sizzle of the kiss run through her, that they fit together so perfectly?

Ryan felt Zoe shiver in response to his kiss. When he felt her go weak in his arms his heart bumped in his chest. A man could lose his reason, Ryan thought, a man could lose his soul, staring into those emerald-green eyes.

A lock of hair fell toward her cheek and she brushed it back absently. Her lips curved in a smile that he recognized as purely feminine.

He told himself not to touch her, but couldn't keep from brushing a fingertip down her cheek. "Zoe, look at me. Tell me what you're thinking, what you're feeling."

Zoe opened her eyes, locked her gaze with his. "That your kisses are lethal," she said, trying hard to keep her voice steady. "I…I have…have to remember to breathe before I faint."

Ryan had tried hard to keep them from entering deep and troublesome waters but knew he was losing the battle.

He wasn't ready to deal with all the emotion he could hear in her voice, see in her eyes. Since the day she'd stepped back into his life all he'd allowed himself to see was a woman who'd been too polished, too savvy and too sophisticated. Never the woman for him.

But here she was, approachable, vulnerable and

touchingly unsure of herself or her charms. He cared
for Zoe too much to ever hurt her again.

He knew what a woman like Zoe wanted, needed.
She needed a man who was emotionally free to make
a total commitment. And right now Ryan wasn't that
man.

He'd tried to tell her. He'd tried to show her. He
wanted her friendship, needed it, for making peace
with Zoe was helping him make peace with himself.

Then she spoke the words he didn't want to hear.
"I love you. I want us to be together."

He eased away gently—just enough to keep the
conversation friendly, the atmosphere teasing, and
their fragile relationship on the track *he'd* chosen for
it.

"There's some powerful chemistry at work here,"
he said.

Zoe heard the flippancy in Ryan's voice. He was
pulling back emotionally. Again. She couldn't understand how he could kiss her senseless one moment
and hold her at arm's length the next.

If only she could convince him that she'd always
be there for him. She could see he didn't want to hear
the words, even though they came from her heart.
Taking a cue from his tone, she said, "I also remember that you flunked chemistry and had to repeat it in
summer school."

They looked at each other, and the tension that had
been building still danced around them.

Ryan's eyes glimmered with an emotion she
couldn't read. "Sex. Lust. Not love. And with just a

kiss we manage to send each other into sensual overload.''

Zoe's heart lurched. But she wasn't going to let him see how much he'd hurt her. Again. She placed her palm on his chest and with mock sternness said, ''I trust you'll be able to control yourself.''

He caught her hand, kissed her palm. ''You test my limits. I'll admit that I want you, body and soul. I'll take you to bed, if that's what you want. If that's what you're ready for. But I can't, I won't, promise you won't be hurt. We'll make love, but we won't mention love.''

''I understand.'' But she didn't. Not really. She knew she loved him truly, madly, deeply and forever. Her heart might be willing to accept whatever he might offer, but her head knew better. Still, she loved him so much she was willing to bet her future he felt the same way—even if he didn't realize it yet.

''I wonder if you do,'' he murmured as he led her back into the restaurant. He looked like he wanted to kiss her, but he held back. ''We'll talk later tonight. We have some big decisions to make.''

''Zoe, you've got a phone call. Long-distance.'' The hostess pointed to a door marked Private. ''You can take it in there.''

Zoe stepped into the office and closed the door. Who could be calling her here? She picked up the phone and punched the flashing button. ''Hello?''

''Zoe, it's Patricia. Don't you check your messages? I've been leaving them all day.'' Why was her producer calling from New York? Zoe glanced at her watch. Less than five minutes until her special was scheduled to air. Her heart dropped into her stomach. Something must have gone wrong.

"I don't have my cell phone with me." Zoe felt the dread spread throughout her body. Something was dreadfully wrong. "How did you find me?"

"How many restaurants can there be in a small town like Riverview?" Patricia asked.

"Riverbend," Zoe automatically corrected. Despite the fact Patricia produced a morning news/entertainment show that was number one in Middle America, she was one of those native New Yorkers who didn't believe life really existed west of the Hudson River. And nothing Zoe said seemed to change her mind.

"Anyway," Patricia continued, "for the first time in network history the VPs for news and entertainment have actually agreed on something."

"What's that?" Here it comes. Zoe steeled herself for what was sure to be bad news.

"Haven't you been listening to a word I've been saying?" Patricia demanded somewhat crossly. "They love your special. They watched it together this afternoon and they loved it!"

Zoe felt herself go weak in the knees. "They loved it? Together?"

"When you get back to New York…you are coming back on Monday, right? Do you have to apply for a get-out-of-Riverbend-free card?"

Zoe's head was spinning as she nodded into the receiver. "Monday. Sure. Of course."

"They've got a big meeting planned." Patricia's voice rose in excitement. "They've got plans for you…plans for us. Gotta go. I'm being beeped. It's been like this all day." *Click.*

Zoe stared at the phone a few seconds before placing it back in its cradle. She took a deep breath to steady herself. The network vice presidents loved her special. They had big plans for her.

She sank into a chair. Her stock was rising at the network. For a moment she let her imagination run free and saw herself as a top network anchor, a major talent who traveled all around the globe reporting serious news stories, not just those glitzy entertainment ones. She'd be reporting news, and maybe making some news along the way.

Ryan would be so proud of her. She slowly leaned back into the chair. The smile filling her face turned into a frown. He would be proud of her, wouldn't he? Suddenly feeling chilled to the bone, Zoe dropped into a chair wrapped her arms around herself.

Less than an hour ago she'd told Ryan she loved him and wanted to spend the rest of her life with him. She was even willing to start a physical relationship with him, because she was so sure of her love for him.

Ryan was the man who meant everything to her. Did he matter more than her career? Of course he did. Being with him, sharing her life with him was more important than her becoming a celebrity. *Because without him, she was only half of whom she was meant to be.*

She had to find him, tell him that she heard the network had big plans for her and that she needed his advice. It seemed that they had a lot of big decisions to make that night.

Zoe saw him standing on the terrace. Thinking Ryan was alone she quickened her pace. And came to a dead stop when she saw Kate step into his arms. Saw Kate smile up at him and Ryan return that smile. Kate rested her head against Ryan's chest and he wrapped his arms around her.

They looked so perfect together. And while she knew in her heart that there was nothing between Ryan and Kate other than friendship, her mind unexpectedly was filled with all those old feelings of abandonment and the pain of not belonging to anyone.

Zoe's lips quivered, her eyes started to fill with tears that she briskly brushed away. She wasn't going to cry. ''They're friends,'' she murmured to herself. ''He's concerned about her, the way I am. It doesn't mean anything…. So why do I feel there's a hole in my heart the size of Manhattan?''

She didn't want to see an intimacy between Kate and Ryan, but it was there nonetheless. And despite all her hopes, her dreams, she couldn't count on having the future with Ryan that she dreamed of. She could have sex with him, but it would be meaningless if she didn't have his love as well. She straightened her shoulders. She hardened her heart. She listened to what her little voice was whispering. *She could have her brilliant career.* She wasn't dependent on Ryan for that.

She stood in the shadows and watched Kate and

Ryan leave together and felt what was left of her heart break into a million pieces.

Not ready to go home, Zoe walked up and down Main Street, searching for answers to questions that had no easy answers. She loved Ryan. Could he, would he, ever love her? She knew he wanted her. And that he needed her. But his heart remained a prisoner of his past, the way her heart had been—and in some ways still was—a prisoner of hers.

She wouldn't deny she craved the spotlight that came with being a correspondent on a national TV news/entertainment program. If she couldn't count on the people she loved to love her back, she'd relied on knowing there were millions of people watching her every morning.

But she knew in her heart and felt deep in her soul that it wasn't enough. That the friendships, the acquaintances, even the few romantic relationships she'd allowed herself, hadn't filled the lonely spots in her life.

She continued walking until she'd reached her street and stopped in front of Ryan's house. The lights were out. It was long after midnight but Zoe was tempted to knock on the door because she wanted to have that conversation he'd promised her.

Or maybe not.

It had been Kate he'd taken home, Kate he'd comforted. Zoe slowly walked up to his front porch and slid bonelessly onto the top step and leaned her head back against the railing. She heard Chance bark, then scratch at the front door.

If Ryan came outside, what would she say to him? And when she went home, what could she say to Kate?

The lights blazed throughout the house next door. She wanted to share with her sister that she always had loved Ryan, had never stopped loving him.

But what stopped her was recalling the happy look on Kate's face when she gazed up at Ryan. Zoe's little voice asked a little bit maliciously, did Kate want Ryan back? It was a thought so idiotic, so preposterous, that Zoe entertained it for but a moment because she was feeling so vulnerable.

But still, the thought lingered like smoke in the air, until finally Zoe stood and walked across the yard and up the steps to Kate's front door. She turned the key and went inside.

From the front hallway she saw Kate curled up on the couch, and started to call out to her. But Zoe hesitated when she saw the phone pressed to Kate's ear and that her sister was crying.

Her own emotions in turmoil, Zoe hurried up the stairs, briskly rubbing her arms to ward off the chill that had enveloped her.

She stripped off her clothes, took a hot shower then donned her nightshirt and slipped into bed, pulling up the comforter so it covered her up to her chin.

The soft breeze coming through the bedroom window should have relaxed her, but it didn't. She felt anxious, unsettled. Her body shifted restlessly on the bed, her heart beat rapidly in her chest.

The slam of a car door jolted her upright. She heard footsteps on the walk, and the front door open, then close. A deep, soothing male voice calling out for Kate. She recognized that voice. It belonged to Ryan.

Ryan had just spent the better part of the evening listening to Kate and Alec alternately expressing doubts about their upcoming marriage. Just nerves, he'd told them both. He'd been so uncomfortable and not too successful in dealing with Kate's tears at the rehearsal dinner, and then pouring a slightly inebriated Alec into bed, that he'd almost forgotten the message he had for Zoe.

Now Kate had asked for him again. He pulled into his driveway, got out of the car, slammed the door and promised himself as he crossed over to Kate's yard and up the steps to her front door that once this wedding was over he was never going to be anyone's best man again. That he was going to take as much time as he needed to figure out what he was going to do with the rest of his life.

Ryan sighed and attempted to scrub the tiredness from his face. He was frustrated because lost in all the end-of-the-evening chaos was the time he'd promised to spend with Zoe.

He opened the front door and saw Kate curled up on the couch, sleeping, with the phone still in her hand.

He'd always been there for Kate. But who did he have to turn to? And then it hit Ryan like a bolt of lightning. It was Zoe who'd been there for him when he'd needed to talk about Sean's death. Zoe, whom he'd chosen to share the news about his new home and his new puppy. She was more than his childhood friend. She'd grown into the perfect woman for the man he'd become.

And he loved her beyond all reason.

A creak of the stairs had him turning and looking up the stairs and into Zoe's eyes. The hurt he saw chilled his blood.

"I waited for you, but you seemed to have time tonight for everyone but me." She turned and ran up the steps.

Ryan chased after her. He grabbed for her arm but she shrugged him loose at the top of the stairs. "I love you with all my heart."

"You're a little too late." The defiant look in her eye had him stepping back.

"I'm here now." He reached out to stroke her cheek and tried to check the desperation he heard in his voice. "C'mon, let's go next door, we'll walk the dog, we can talk all we want. Zoe, I want us to be together."

"You're a little late," she repeated sadly. She eased away and moved over to the doorway to her room. Her voice was cool, but the quiver in her lips showed she wasn't in as much control as she'd like for him to believe. And that gave him hope.

"But you love me." Ryan tried to beat back the unfamiliar panic rising from his gut to his heart.

"I do love you, Ryan, but I don't see much of a future for us. You're still beating yourself up over Sean's death. That you couldn't do more, be more. You're not Superman, Ryan, you're just a man."

"I can't change who I am, what I believe in, Zoe, not even for you."

"And I can't pretend that I'm not hurt whenever I think of you and Kate together."

"You're acting like a coward, hiding behind that so-called New York City sophistication. At the first little chink in your yellow-brick road you run and hide."

"Well," she said quietly. "Now I know what you truly think about me. So it's good we had this little talk. And after the wedding, we won't have any reason to see each other again."

She closed the door.

Ryan stood there a few moments before he started down the stairs. He paused at the front door before taking the stairs up again, two at a time.

He banged on her bedroom door. "Tomorrow after the wedding we're going to deal with each other."

Chapter Ten

The trip down the aisle seemed to be taking longer than Zoe remembered from the past night's rehearsal. She clutched the tea-rose bouquet tightly in both hands and counted softly to herself as she walked steadily down the white satin ribbon draped over the wood floor.

She watched her feet rather than the scene around her but felt all the people in the packed chapel watching every move she made. Step and one and step and two and step and three....

"Zoe...Zoe...Zoe..." She looked up abruptly and saw Ryan beckon to her from the front of the chapel. She quickened her pace, stumbled and then was amazed to feel herself rise several inches off the floor and float the rest of the way to where he stood.

Her feet hit the satin-covered aisle with a thump. What was going on? Ryan wore a white tux, and a shiny gold sheriff's star was pinned in place of a boutonniere. Low on his hips rode—could that be?—an empty holster.

She wanted to believe this scene was nothing more than a bad dream, but it appeared all too real. *Wake up. Wake up,* she told herself.

Zoe heard murmurs from the guests in the pews, and tried turning her head to the right, then to the left, but some unknown force kept her in place. The minister, wearing rimless spectacles and dressed in a black topcoat with extra-long tails, looked down his long nose at her.

"Do you, Zoe Russell," he intoned in a deep baritone voice, "promise to dedicate the rest of your natural life to the needs and whims of *Wake Up, America,* forsaking all others, including," he pointed to Ryan, "the man whose love you've so *callously* tossed away?"

Zoe shivered. She tried to step back, but her feet were glued to the satin ribbon.

"You, Zoe Russell, will live the rest of your natural life *alone*—" the minister shuddered in distaste and the room filled with all those nameless, faceless people shuddered along with him "—all alone in a tiny studio apartment in New York City."

Ryan stepped forward and held out his arms, but instead of wrapping them around her he stepped right through her as though he was a ghost. Something cold and clammy slobbered all over her face and Zoe pushed at it helplessly.

She screamed, bolted upright and faced her tormentor.

"Chance." She was in her bed and it had been just a dream. She stroked the puppy's silky fur. "How did you get in?"

Her heart continued to beat wildly in her chest and Zoe took a few deep breaths to calm down. Chance placed his front paws right in the middle of her chest before barking happily and settling in her lap.

Zoe glanced at the clock on the nightstand. It was shortly past noon and she was running late.

"You've got a lot to do today, a lot to think about," Zoe muttered to herself as she tossed back the bedcovers and tumbled the puppy, who chewed at a piece of paper attached to his collar, onto her pillows.

She played a quick game of tug-of-war with Chance, finally wrestling the paper away from the playful puppy.

"Please give us a chance." She sighed as she recognized Ryan's scrawl. He knew her soft spots well, and he'd obviously brought Chance over in a gesture of peace.

She wanted to forgive him. She only hoped he would forgive her.

Last night he'd said he loved her. He'd been in a fit of panic when he'd said the words, but Zoe had to believe they'd come from his heart.

She loved Ryan. That she knew, just as she knew he loved her, too.

But something had gone dreadfully wrong last night. She'd been hurting, but it had been foolish and childish for her to lash out at Ryan. Now she was unsure how to repair the damage. She only knew she had to.

Zoe hurried through her shower. She carefully applied her makeup before stepping into her bridesmaid dress. She stared at her unhappy reflection in the mirror and shook her head to clear it. She was going to fight for Ryan. She loved him. She wanted to marry him. ''Thrice a bridesmaid and never a bride. That's *not* going to be me.''

She glanced at the clock and moaned. Less than an hour before the ceremony was scheduled to begin. But if she was quick, she could make it to the church with a few minutes to spare before Kate started her walk down the aisle without her maid of honor.

Zoe flew down the stairs and out the door. Ryan had called her a coward. But she wasn't. Before the wedding was over, she was going to prove to him just how wrong he was.

Ryan punched out the numbers on his cell phone and listened as the voice mail kicked in once again. Where could Zoe be? The wedding was due to begin—he glanced at his watch—in mere minutes and he was frantic that something had happened to her.

He'd paced the short walkway outside the front of the church so many times over the past hour, he was sure he'd worn down a layer of brick. He was about ready to call Jake and have him patrol the town's streets for her when Zoe suddenly turned the corner and halted at the edge of the brick walkway.

She ruffled her fingers through her hair, then

ran her hands up and down her dress to rid it of the wrinkles.

Ryan's heart beat a tattoo. She looked out of breath, but absolutely radiant. He was never so relieved to see anyone, or so furious she'd almost missed her sister's wedding. He loved her more than he had ever loved anyone before. And once he finished throttling her, he'd tell her so. Again and again until he was hoarse from saying the words.

"Where have you been?" He held open the door and followed her into the church.

"I have something to say to you."

"Later." He not so gently pushed her into the vestibule and through a door marked Private just as the organ rang out with the first chords of the traditional wedding march.

Now that she was at the church, Zoe was impatient for the wedding to begin and to end. If she'd arrived just a few minutes earlier, she would have had time to talk with Ryan.

But maybe it was better this way. After the reception they could make their excuses and find a place alone so they could talk and sort out their problems.

Even though they had said they loved each other, there was so much emotional baggage piled up between them they might not be able to find a way to be together. And if that happened, Zoe knew that as unhappy as she'd be, she wasn't going to leave Riverbend until she had at least salvaged their friendship.

Then she could return alone to New York, to *Wake Up, America*, and to the life she'd thought she wanted. A life that wouldn't be complete unless she shared it with Ryan.

"I'm sorry I'm late." Zoe hugged Kate. "Are you okay?"

"Yes, now that you're here. I'd wondered though," Kate joked, "if you'd hightailed it back to New York."

"I promised to see you happily married first." Zoe lightly pinched Kate's cheeks to give them some additional color.

"I was really nervous last night," Kate said with a teary smile. "I kept wondering if marrying Alec was a mistake."

"But you love him," Zoe said quietly. She thought about how much she loved Ryan. "And you know that Alec loves you. That's what's important."

"I know." Kate paused then asked frantically, "Where's my borrowed and blue?"

Zoe took Kate's hand, where she placed a light blue garter into her palm. "Here's your blue, with love."

She tucked a lace handkerchief that had belonged to their grandmother into a fold of Kate's wedding gown. "And your borrowed, from Grandma."

With a small smile, Zoe brushed away the tears that threatened to spill onto her sister's cheek.

Kate wrapped her in a big hug. "I love you, Zoe. And don't worry, Ryan will come around. I guarantee it."

"There's no end to your matchmaking, is there?" Zoe said dryly. She opened the door where their father stood waiting, and pushed Kate through it. "I love you, too. Be happy."

Lawrence offered Kate one hand and Zoe the other. Zoe grasped her father's hand and squeezed it. On impulse, she wrapped her arms around his neck and hugged him. Then she took her place and started down the aisle.

Zoe tried to concentrate on the wedding ceremony, but she couldn't keep her gaze off Ryan. She smiled at the way his brows rose when Alec turned to him and begged frantically for the ring to place on Kate's finger. She wanted to trace Ryan's lips as his mouth curved in a sexy smile when the bride and groom exchanged their first kiss as husband and wife.

And she found herself never wanting to let go of him when he purposefully offered Zoe his hand as they followed the newly married couple back down the aisle.

She was thinking about how best to apologize to him when Kate suddenly stopped halfway down the aisle and turned. With a look of pure glee on her face, Kate took a few steps back and tossed her bridal bouquet over Zoe's head and into Ryan's hands.

He looked down at the bouquet, then up at Kate, before he finally turned to Zoe, who stared back at him in disbelief.

"Gotcha!" Kate laughed and clapped her hands. "I've been waiting *years* to do that!"

Ryan's lips curved and the smile reached his eyes. "And I've been waiting for what seems like years to do *this*."

He reached for Zoe and she found herself picked up and turned upside down, her hips resting on his left shoulder, the blood rushing to her head.

"Put me down!" she ordered. "You're making a spectacle."

"What do you all say? Should I put her down?" Ryan asked as he slowly turned in a circle before the assembled guests.

"No!" they shouted in unison.

"Yes!" She struggled but he kept a tight grip on her.

Ryan whispered into Zoe's ear. "The public has spoken."

She raised her head and saw her parents smiling. "Do something. Make him put me down."

Lawrence's eyes danced with laughter. "I'm not going to tangle with the law in Riverbend. I'm confident you two can work it out."

Ryan kept one hand lightly on her derriere to keep her in place. "Excuse us," he said politely to Kate and Alec. "We'll join you later. We have some personal business to take care of."

He carefully leaned over and picked up the bouquet that he'd dropped and thrust it into Zoe's hands. "Hold this."

With those words, Ryan walked the rest of the way down the aisle, through the chapel and out the church doors. He paused on the brick walkway. "Let's see... Where to?"

Zoe clutched the wedding bouquet with one hand and pounded on his back with the other. "If you know what's good for you, you'll take me back inside the church where you can apologize...to me...in front of everyone."

He shook his head and the motion had Zoe's head

spinning. He shifted her body carefully on his shoulder. "You're a little heavy, but I think we can make it."

"I'll have you arrested!"

Ryan started walking, and felt Zoe brace her hands against his back to keep herself from flopping around. "So, what did you want to say to me?"

"There is nothing, absolutely nothing I have to say to you that you'd want to hear." Her voice was like ice.

Ryan smiled to himself. Oh, he liked her best when she was feisty. And if he had his way, he'd be dealing with her style of feisty the rest of his life. "Oh, I'm sure you'll have plenty to say to me, and it will be what I want to hear. Pretty diabolical of Kate to toss me that bouquet, wasn't it?"

"I'll deal with my sister after I make mincemeat of you."

She kicked her legs and Ryan barely managed to keep the toe of her shoe from connecting with a very personal part of his anatomy.

"Watch it," he admonished her. "You might damage the next generation of O'Connors."

"I know exactly what I'm doing. Where are you taking me? Ryan, this is kidnapping!"

"It's not kidnapping," he pointed out mildly. "I had everyone's approval."

"Not mine." She sounded grumpy, but at least she'd stopped kicking him.

He chuckled and patted her gently on the rump. "I had your father's. And that's good enough for me."

Zoe groaned. The minute he put her down she'd

give him a piece of her mind. How dare he embarrass her, then abduct her, in full daylight, in front of all the wedding guests.

She might love him more than she could have ever imagined, but no way was he going to treat her like a piece of baggage. And she told him so, right as he carried her through the front door of the Riverbend Police Department, where the dispatcher desk sat empty, and down the hallway to the jail area.

She stiffened in his arms. "You wouldn't dare!"

He kicked open the jail door and dropped her unceremoniously onto the cot. It was as lumpy as she'd remembered. When she tried to get up he gently pressed his hand to her shoulder to keep her in place.

Ryan stepped back and kicked the door shut.

Zoe winced as she heard the key fall from the lock onto the cement floor.

The sound echoed loudly, but Ryan didn't seem the least bit concerned. "It's the only spot in town," he said, "where we can be guaranteed some privacy."

"It's the only spot in town no one would think to look for us." The bridal bouquet slid out of her hand.

"Exactly." Ryan put it in her lap and sat next to her. In a movement so quick Zoe had no time to react, he clasped handcuffs around both their wrists. "We'll stay locked in here together until you see reason."

"I can't believe you did that." She stared at their wrists, locked together.

"No? What about this?" With his free hand, he took a key out of his pants pocket and she watched, still in disbelief, as he leaned back and tossed it over his head in the direction of the tiny barred window.

The key hit the metal and then clanged to the pavement outside.

"That was real smart, Slick. No one's out front. No one knows we're here. And you've managed to not only lock us up together, you've locked *us* together." Zoe yanked her hand throwing Ryan off balance so his head ended up in her lap.

With her free hand, she pushed him off her and they both went tumbling off the cot and onto the floor like two rag dolls.

"That," Ryan said as he shoved her elbow away from his windpipe, "was the general idea."

She raised their chained wrists. "That our relationship should come to this."

"It doesn't have to be this way," Ryan said softly. He cupped her chin and turned her to face him.

And what she saw in his eyes gave her hope. They were smiling at her, laughing with her and filled with love for her. She'd given him enough sass. She considered another round of Truth or Dare, but decided there had been too much game-playing between them over the past weeks. But still, she couldn't resist tweaking him just a little. "I've been doing some detective work."

"Have you now." He drew her closer. "You've been so busy running toward me, then away from me, that I'm surprised you found the time."

"Pay attention," she said with mock sternness. "A man doesn't purchase his childhood home, fill it with well-worn but well-loved mementos and add a puppy to the mix unless he's planning to stay put for a long while."

"And from this you've concluded?"

"That you love Riverbend and you've decided to take the mayor up on his offer to continue as police chief. And…" Zoe paused.

"Go on," Ryan urged.

"Whether you realize it or not, you're coming to terms with Sean's death. You're moving on with your life."

"I bet you're going to tell me that you knew I was staying put before I did."

Zoe smiled. "You're not a quitter, you've never been a coward." Her smile dimmed. She brushed a tear from her eye.

Ryan caught her hand, brought it to his lips, then down to his heart. "I'm sorry for what I said yesterday. You're no coward. You're one of the bravest people I know. It took guts to leave Riverbend, move up to New York alone, and end up on top."

"You were right about me," Zoe said sadly. "I wasted so much energy trying to ignore the past that I almost let the present, and the future, slip by me. Being on top of the heap isn't important if it means I'm standing there all by myself. And I don't want to stand alone anymore."

"What about that meeting with the network bigwigs?"

Zoe looked startled. "Who told you?"

"Your persistent producer left messages all over town," Ryan said dryly, "including one at the station, last night. I would have given it to you sooner, but Kate was in a tizzy over something Alec said, and I rushed over to your house to try and calm her down and forgot to deliver the message to you.''

"So you already know…"

"That the network has big plans for you. You're a talented young woman. I'm very proud of what you've accomplished, and I'd never stand in your way. Last night, when you stood on the stairway and looked at me so coldly, told me it was over between us before it had really begun, it shook me to the core. I couldn't bear the thought of losing you again.''

She touched her brow to his. "I love you, Ryan, more than I ever believed I could love. If the network wants me that bad, it will have to make some concessions.''

"Whatever decisions we make, we'll make them together. You're the most important person in my life. I love you, Zoe. You somehow managed to rip off my emotional blinders without me even realizing it. With you by my side, I don't think there's anything I couldn't do. That we couldn't do together.''

And then he drew her closer, and kissed her. His lips touched hers, and Zoe felt all the tension, all the uncertainty leave her body, replaced by that wonderful melting feeling only Ryan could provide.

She lost herself in his kiss, and kissed him back with all the love in her heart, in her soul. Ryan was right. Together they were an unstoppable team. Except… "We still have a few problems to iron out. Like who's going to walk the puppy.''

Ryan gazed at the woman he loved more than life itself. No matter how old they were, he would never tire of seeing those sparkling green eyes shine with love for him.

"We'll walk the puppy together. Together we'll write a lifetime contract. No negotiation there," Ryan said with a confidence that brought a smile to her lips. "With the number, and the timing, of our offspring to be discussed in the very near future."

"Sex?" Zoe asked with all the innocence she could muster.

"As soon as I get my ring on your finger," Ryan growled and hugged her to him.

"I meant the sex of our children," she said with a smile.

"Sons and daughters," he said, "We'll raise our children the way our parents raised us. With love."

She heard a door open.

"Zoe? Ryan?" It was a male voice she didn't recognize.

"Where could they be?" Another voice, this one female.

She started to call out, only to find Ryan's hand dart across her mouth. She pried it loose. "What are you doing? Whoever's there can let us out."

"Don't let them know we're here."

"Are you crazy? We might not get out of here for days."

"Would that be so bad?" The laughter in his voice had her narrowing her gaze on him.

She pretended to consider, before saying, "Well, maybe not."

"Good." He dug deep into his pocket and pulled out another key. "I'm madly in love with you, but not crazy enough to lock us in here without having some way of getting out.''

He started to fit the key into the cuffs, but Zoe grabbed his hand, and plucked the key out of it, safely tucking it away in the bodice of her dress.

He grinned and started to reach for her.

She grinned, too, and pulled back just enough to look at the man who was all hers. He was still the one. The only one.

Their life together, she decided as she drew him to her for a kiss that they'd both long remember, was going to be just...perfect.

*   *   *   *   *

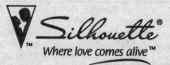

COMING NEXT MONTH

#1660 WITH HIS KISS—Laurey Bright
He was back in town! Gunther "Steve" Stevens had always unsettled Triss Allerdyce—and he'd been secretly jealous of her marriage to his much older mentor. But now her husband's will brought them together again, and Steve's anger soon turned to love. But would that be enough to awaken the hidden passions of this Sleeping Beauty?

#1661 THE WEDDING ADVENTURE—Melissa McClone
The *last* thing Cade Armstrong Waters wanted to do was spend two weeks on a tropical island with socialite Cynthia Sterling! But with his charity organization at stake, he agreed to the crazy scheme. Surviving Cynthia's passionate kisses with his heart intact was another story....

#1662 THE NANNY SOLUTION—Susan Meier
Daycare Dads
Nanny Hannah Evans was going to give millionaire Jake Malloy a piece of her mind! It was bad enough the sexy single father was running around like a government spy, but now she was actually falling for her confounding boss. Was he *ever* going to give up his secret double life for fatherhood and...love?

#1663 THE KNIGHT'S KISS—Nicole Burnham
Soulmates
Thanks to a medieval curse, Nick Black had been around for a long time...a *long* time. Researching ancient artifacts for Princess Isabella diTalora, he hoped to find the answers to break the spell. But would he find the one woman who could break the walls around his heart?

#1664 CAPTIVATING A COWBOY—Jill Limber
So city girl Julie Kerns broke her collarbone trying to fix up her grandmother's cottage—she could *hire* someone to help, right? But what if he was ex-Navy SEAL Tony Graham—a man sexy as sin who kissed like heaven? Maybe that cottage would need *a lot* more work than she first thought....

#1665 THE BACHELOR CHRONICLES—Lissa Manley
Jared Warfield was torn between his pride in his business and the need for privacy to adopt his orphaned baby niece. So he planned to show fiesty reporter Erin James all about the store—and nothing about himself. But the best-laid plans went awry when the unlikely couple finally met!

SRCNM0403